Coming Out

A Novella

Coming Out

A Novella by
J.T. McDaniel

C.E.B. Pubs
Dublin, Ohio

Coming Out

Based upon the stage play, *Coming Out: A Dark Comedy in Two Acts*, by J.T. McDaniel. Stage play © 2013, by J.T. McDaniel, published by Riverdale Books.

For information on performance rights for the play, you may contact:
Riverdale Literary Holdings, Inc.
P.O. Box 3716
Dublin, Ohio 43016
or apply online using the forms to be found at http://jtmcdaniel.com, http://comingouttheplay.com, or http://cpctheatrical.com.

ISBN: 978-1-943288-12-0

For the Victims

I

GORDON FULLER SAT THOUGHTFULLY ON THE SIDE OF Bob Anderson's desk, looking out the window at the back of Miller Hall. He would have to walk over there shortly, where 237 pre-Med students would be waiting to hear him expound on modern genetics. As modern as he could manage, he thought. Things changed at such a frantic rate these days he was hard put to keep up. Was junk DNA still junk, or had someone figured out what some of it did, and now he'd have to change his lectures for the fourth time this year?

He found himself envying Bob. The Oxford educated philosophy professor had managed to pick a subject that hadn't changed that much in the last thousand years. He turned out a book every three or four years, as often as not just making the same arguments he'd made in the last one, and didn't have to worry about some newly minted PhD coming up with something that would make much of his education obsolete. Plato was still Plato and Aristotle was still Aristotle, and if they were both wrong about a lot of things, even that didn't really change.

The Limey bastard was happily married, too, which Fuller found nearly as annoying as a discipline that allowed him to use the same lectures for years.

"Forty years, huh?"

"Indeed."

Fuller shook his head. "You know, we're the same age, and I've had four wives."

Bob smiled. "I expect one day you'll find the right one."

"After the last one, I'm sticking to genetics. At a purely academic level."

Bob reached into his left vest pocket and pulled out his watch. It was a Hamilton 992B, one of the lever-set, railroad certified models that company was famous for. The watch had been 30 years old when his father gave it to him to mark his admission to Oxford in 1968, after a brief, injury-terminated stint in the Special Air Service, and it still kept excellent time 44 years later. Not as accurate as a quartz movement might, but it could still pass a railroad timekeeper's test if it had to. Railroad watches had to be accurate to within 30 seconds a week, and his gained at about half that rate. "A good, American watch," his father had said. "Not one of those cheap Swiss things."

His father was a bit of a snob.

"I suppose," Bob said, "that I should be getting home. My children should start arriving around one o'clock."

"Only good thing out of those four marriages of mine," Fuller grunted. "The kids all turned out okay." He had four children, three from his first marriage and another from his second. Two physicians, a civil engineer, and a not quite best-selling novelist.

Bob pushed his chair back from his desk and stood. He was a tall man, his silver hair cut very short on the sides and back. There was so little on top that he found it more practical to shave off the few remaining hairs. Better to admit being bald than to attempt to disguise the fact with some silly comb over, or a bad toupée. It didn't exactly make him look like a starship captain—and why did a Frenchman speak with a British accent?—but he had to admit that Patrick Stewart had influenced his tonsorial preferences. Bald on top with shoulder length hair, he thought, looked just as silly as most other alternatives.

He felt that he looked quite good for a man of 64. Not

quite as slim as he once was, but not really overweight, either. His house was just off campus, so he generally walked the mile and a half to and from work each day, which no doubt helped keep his weight under control. His eyesight was still good enough he needed glasses only for reading.

Relaxing in his office after his last class of the day, he was wearing dark trousers, highly polished cap-toe shoes, a medium blue, long sleeved shirt, charcoal vest, and a bow tie. He'd been wearing bow ties for years, and had dozens in his closet. More often than not he wore either the dark and sky blue Eton stripe, or the crested blue of Balliol College, Oxford, where he had earned his Doctor of Philosophy degree. Today he'd picked a plain burgundy tie, and he'd been sorry he had about halfway through his class.

He walked over to the coat rack in the corner and put on his jacket. The Harris tweed, with the leather elbow patches, made him look like a college professor, which seemed appropriate. It was nearly a uniform for him after all these years.

I dress like my father, he thought. I dress like an Englishman, and I've lived in Ohio for 38 years and been an American for the last 30 of them.

"So did mine," he said. "My kids all turned out nicely." He laughed suddenly. "Well, Jim's a con artist, but otherwise…"

"I thought Jim was a preacher."

"Same thing."

Bob started out of the office and Fuller followed. In the outer office Carol Burgess looked up from a stack of paperwork on her desk.

"You may as well go home," Bob told her. "I won't be coming back today."

"Okay, thanks, Professor. I've got something I want to do, and I may as well get it done early."

"See you tomorrow."

The two men walked out into the corridor.

"I'll see you later, Bob," Fuller said, turning toward the left.

"Later."

Bob turned to the right, toward the main entrance. He walked out of the building, glancing up at the sky. A few high cumulus clouds, cotton white, seemed to promise fair weather. The temperature was in the low 70s. Bob had moved to Ohio before the UK started to get fussy about using Celsius, so he continued to think in Fahrenheit.

As usual, he'd walked to work today. He'd been walking for the last 38 years, ever since he started teaching at the little central Ohio liberal arts college. He only drove if the weather was bad.

The weather was just fine today.

Walking gave him time to think. He might have to stop and speak with a student, or another professor, but there was still very little to occupy his mind. He didn't have to worry about operating a car, or wonder what someone would do at the next corner.

Perhaps, he thought, it's simply that I'm still in some essential way British, even after all these years. His next door neighbor also taught at the college, and he drove every day. That was the American thing to do, drive. His neighbor would get into his car to drive half a block to buy something at the convenience store on the corner. Bob didn't think it was worth starting the engine if he was going less than a mile. Not if he didn't need to carry something heavy.

He was still British. The British walked, Americans drove.

II

PROFESSOR ROBERT ARTHUR GORDON LLOYD ANDERSON, DPhil., called "Bob" by nearly everyone, took his key ring from his left front trouser pocket, sorted through the keys, found the one he needed, and was starting to insert it into the lock when the door opened.

"I saw you coming up the walk," his wife said, putting her arms around him and tilting her head up to be kissed. Bob, being a cold, aloof Englishman, naturally did exactly that. He'd been kissing this woman upon his return home every day for the last 40 years. He found that he still enjoyed it very much.

"How was your class?" Susan Morton Anderson asked.

"Boring. I need to write a new lecture."

Susan looked at him doubtfully. She thought he was probably right, but didn't think he'd do it. He wrote books, not lectures. The lectures he recycled, year after year.

She had long since realized that in some ways her husband was rather lazy. He was the stable one; the one who never changed.

"Ready for the family?" she asked, closing the door behind them.

Bob took out his watch and checked the time. "Not much choice, is there? They'll all be here soon enough."

"Naturally. We'll only have one fortieth anniversary."

"I remember that day." And not, he thought, anywhere nearly as fondly as his wife seemed to. "Standing in line at the

5

registry office in Oxford. Filling out all the paperwork. Dealing with our friends. Getting signatures from the witnesses. And finally the clerk making the whole thing official."

"Don't forget the second wedding after we came here."

Bob frowned. "How could I? We'd been married for two years by then. You were pregnant with Jim. But your Mum just wouldn't consider us properly married unless her minister mumbled something over us in her church."

Susan slipped her arm around her husband's waist, leaning her head on his shoulder. "You cooperated better than I ever expected you to on that one," she said. "I knew perfectly well a Methodist ceremony wasn't going to mean anything to you."

"It meant something to your mother." And I did not want to get on her bad side, he thought. Neither Clytemnestra nor Medea had anything on that woman.

"It would have been more interesting," he went on, "had my dad been there. He'd no doubt have debated the minister as to why there couldn't possibly be a God."

"Something you'd *never* do, of course."

"Not at my own wedding."

He looked at his watch again, then walked over to the bar behind the sofa. He dropped several ice cubes into a glass, then poured in some whisky.

I've been living here too long, he thought. A good single malt and ice cubes. I'm turning into an American. He shrugged. At least I'm not mixing it with Coca Cola.

As he lifted the glass, Susan put her hand on his arm. "You know, Dear, Jim will be here very soon. Are you sure you want to be drinking?"

"If Jim is coming, I particularly want to be drinking. He's a lot easier to take if you're already half pissed."

"Oh, don't say 'pissed'."

"I'm British, my dear. The slang doesn't all fade away, even after spending 38 years in Ohio."

"Sure it doesn't. You can manage to say 'standing in line'

instead of 'queuing,' but an inoffensive euphemism for drunk is just too much for you."

"You should probably be glad I gave up cigarettes, then."

Susan allowed herself to smile. His sense of humor was as British as his accent, and she still loved it after all these years. Besides, he was right. Jim *was* easier to take if you were a bit drunk.

"Well," she said, "if you're going to drink, make one for me, too."

"Bourbon?"

"And ginger ale."

Bob grabbed a glass and the ice tongs and set to work. "You'll have it easy, you know. Jim doesn't spend half his visits telling *you* that you're going to hell when you die."

"He loves his mother. He wants the best for me."

"He's got me roasting for all eternity."

III

THE BIG CADILLAC SUV ROLLED SERENELY DOWN I-71 toward Columbus. Reverend James Anderson was looking straight ahead. Once in a while he would look over at his wife, Karen, who seemed to be dozing as they drove toward his parents' home.

He had a CD from his church inserted in the player. It was one of his favorite hymns. A relatively new one, written by his choir director, and sung by a gospel quartet.

He is coming for me,
He will take me away,
On that wonderful, wonderful day,
And the sinners will cry,
For they know they will die,
And their fate is to burn evermore.
Oh, I know I am saved,
I will be with my Lord,
What joy it will be on that day,
When in rapture I rise,
Free my soul, soar on high,
While the sinners in agony sigh!

How much longer would it be, he wondered? What if it was today? What would it feel like to be lifted up into heaven? It was coming soon, he was sure of that.

"Carl and the boys did a nice job on that song, don't you think?" he said.

Karen turned her head toward him, but continued to lean against the passenger side door. "Huh?"

"The song. It gets the message across."

If the message is that you're going to heaven at the head of the line and the peasants are going to have to suffer for your amusement, it does, Karen thought.

"Very nice," she said. You didn't disagree with Jim. She'd learned that long ago.

Jim glanced at the dashboard clock. "Another 20 minutes, I think," he said. "It'll be good to see Mom." He thought a moment, "Dad, too, I suppose."

"Both your parents are nice."

He shot her a look. "Mom is nice. Dad? Unless he's changed recently, we won't be seeing him in heaven."

IV

BOB HANDED SUSAN HER DRINK. They clinked glasses and took a sip. Neither was really a heavy drinker, though Bob went through the Scotch considerably faster than Susan used up the Bourbon. Both tended to increase their consumption rate when Jim was around, despite the blindingly obvious fact that he absolutely disapproved of alcohol.

"How did Jim turn out that way, anyway?" Susan asked. "Your father's a physics professor. You're a philosophy professor. You're both atheists. So how did Jim end up a mega-church pastor and TV evangelist? How's that work?"

Bob shrugged. "Well, we did let him go to that Bible college, didn't we?"

Susan took another sip. She placed her glass on the bar and began to straighten the pillows on the love seat. "Remember what he was like last year? Insisting everyone call him *Doctor* Anderson?"

Bob took his drink to his easy chair and sat down. He was still wearing his tweed sport coat, and someone might have inferred this to be a left over manifestation of growing up in England. An American would have removed the jacket as soon as he got home. Keeping it on had been ingrained in Bob when he was quite young. It wasn't that the British were more formal, really. It was just that their idea of proper room temperature was significantly cooler. Or had been when he was young.

"Oh, yes. Graduated 15 years ago, so his school gives him an honorary doctor of divinity degree. Lower standards, I suppose. At a good school he'd have to wait 25 years for that."

"I certainly don't insist people call *me* doctor. Well, except for my students, but that's college policy."

"I'm perfectly happy being called professor," Bob said. "Still, I can't help but think that an earned doctorate from Oxford counts for a bit more than an honorary degree from Central Midwest Bible College."

"Don't get into a fight with him, okay?"

Bob chuckled softly. "I'll try not to."

Susan picked up a stack of books from the sofa and moved them to the narrow table behind it. The title of a new hard cover volume caught her eye.

"Jim hates your latest book, you know." She held up the book to emphasize this.

The History of Gods: Essays on the Persistence of Middle Eastern Mythology into Modern Times.

"I really can't imagine why a fundamentalist minister would have a problem with that," Bob grinned.

Susan certainly could. "Besides the general context, you call yourself an atheist in it."

"I am an atheist."

"Jim doesn't like it when you make the declaration. Of course, your father is a lot more confrontational about that than you are, and Jim doesn't complain about his books nearly as much."

"Yes, well... Dad writes physics textbooks. I don't suppose Jim's sort of Christian actually reads those. They don't need physics, they have magic."

"You might consider giving in a little with Jim this time. Don't be so adamant."

"Well, I'm quite sure there's no God, but I'd change my mind if someone could give me real evidence."

"Jim tries."

"Not very well. You don't need God for a spectacular sunset. All you need is planetary rotation, some clouds, and sunlight refracting through them."

"Our son seems to need more."

"Well, he always was a needy sort."

"He just wants proof."

"So do I. We both want proof that God exists. I just have higher standards." He smiled. "Someone recently told me that it isn't actually possible to be an atheist, because it isn't possible to prove God doesn't exist. True enough, I suppose, but you really can't prove he does, either."

Susan picked up her drink from the bar and sat on the arm of the sofa. "I still like the idea of having one. The older I get, the better I like the idea of heaven."

Bob swallowed a bit more of his drink. "You and me for all eternity? Like the Mormons?"

"Bob, we've been married for 40 years, and I love you, but in heaven I'm hoping for Warren Beatty."

Shaking his head, Bob got up and walked to the window, looking out over the front lawn. "Good luck with that one. With our luck, his sister will be right and we'll just wind up right back here again."

"But not necessarily together."

"One can only hope."

Bob could feel his wife's arms circling his waist from behind, saw her face reflected in the window over his shoulder. "Really?" she said. "How much fun would life be with no one to argue with?"

He smiled ironically. "Deadly dull. Still, life can be so frustrating at times. Think of all those lovely young coeds I could have had."

He felt her elbow shoving against his rib cage. "Think of all those you did."

"Oh, mere flirtations, my dear. I can't help being irresistible."

Susan started to walk away, then noticed that her drink was nearly gone. She tilted the glass to her lips and finished it off.

"Yeah, sure you are," she said. Her husband was tall, and reasonably presentable, but he wasn't exactly the leading man type now, and never had been. As cinematic Englishmen went, he'd be more Arthur Treacher than Cary Grant. He sounded more like Richard Burton — presuming Burton had spent the last 38 years living in central Ohio.

She held out her glass. "Let me have another, will you?"

Bob took her glass and walked to the bar, finishing his own as he crossed the room.

"Same?"

Susan nodded. Bob dumped out the old ice and put in fresh cubes from the insulated ice bucket. He poured more Scotch into his glass, measured a shot of Bourbon into his wife's and topped it up with ginger ale. Finished, he carried the drinks across the living room to where Susan was now sitting in her easy chair.

"Here you are."

"Thank you."

"Quite welcome." He took out his watch and checked it. "Nearly one o'clock," he said. "I suppose someone should be arriving soon."

Susan sipped at her drink. "I hope it's George or Ellen first. I'm not sure I'm drunk enough for Jim just yet."

"One never is."

Susan shook her head. It wasn't really Jim she needed to be drunk for, so much as the inevitable clash of father, son, and theology.

She looked up at Bob, standing beside her chair. "Your class was okay today?"

He frowned. "One student did make that annoying comment."

"Which remark? My students make lots of them."

"You know the one. I blame the BBC."

"Someone said you dress like Doctor Who again, didn't they?"

"I don't."

"Yes, you do."

"No, he dresses like me. I was dressing like this when Matt Smith was in nappies."

Susan looked up at her husband. "Forty years ago today we were married," she said.

"I know. I was there, too."

She tugged on the hem of his jacket. "Yes. In that same sport coat, I think."

He looked down at his wife and frowned, shaking his head. "Hardly. I've only had this a few months."

"One just like it, then."

She had him there. He'd been buying his jackets from the same Saville Row tailor since he was at Eton. With most of his family still living in England, it was easy enough to make a visit to his tailor a part of the annual pilgrimage. His shirts, socks, shoes, and underwear were generally American, but his suits, sport coats, trousers, waistcoats, and overcoats were nearly all from his London tailor. He had seven very similar tan Harris tweed sport coats hanging in his closet. He tended to think of them as a form of academic dress.

In America, after all, professors didn't wear robes on a daily basis.

"Oh," he said, "very likely."

"You never really change. You get older, but you don't really change."

"Would you want me to?"

"You could stop dating your students. You're getting too old for that sort of thing."

"I stopped doing that years ago, my love," Bob said, walking behind her chair and leaning over it, resting his elbows on the back. "The rules have changed, you know."

Susan snickered. "Bless those sexual harassment laws, huh?"

"How much have they slowed you down?"

Susan suddenly realized a vase was slightly out of place on the long table behind the sofa. She hopped up and quickly went over to fix it. It should be just this much further to the left, she decided, and the flowers should be turned a bit more toward the center of the room.

"You're not answering."

"Shouldn't the children be here by now? What time is it, anyway?"

Bob took out his watch. "One oh three."

"There, see. They should be here."

> *"Full of wise care is your counsel, madam,*
> *Take all swift advantage of the hours."*

"Well, they *should* be here by now."

Bob glanced at the front window as a big, white SUV pulled into the driveway. "Apparently," he said, "at least one of them is. But I don't recognize the car."

V

THE FRONT DOOR OPENED AND JIM WALKED IN, his wife following. James Anderson was a tall, impressive looking man, dressed in an expensive, conservatively cut gray suit. At 37, his light brown hair was thinning, but a toupee that very likely cost more than a family of four would spend on food and housing for a month disguised the fact. Jim had four of them at home, plus the one he was wearing. If he was going to preach on TV every day, it was important to look youthful, and a full head of hair added to the impression. So did his suits, the cut adding some width to his merely average shoulders. He didn't think of himself as vain. He was presenting an image, one that would impress his congregation and television viewers, and perhaps influence them to listen more closely to what he said.

Karen was dressed in a light blue seersucker suit, the fitted skirt ending decorously just below the knee. Her blond hair was worn up. The look was conservative, appropriate for a preacher's wife. It also made her look older, which was useful, for at 26 she was eleven years younger than her husband. Tall and slender, in a less conservative outfit she might have looked like a show girl, but her husband made sure she kept covered up in properly modest styles. Her job was to complement him, not to stand out on her own.

Susan hurried over. "It's about time someone got here," she said, hugging her son and daughter-in-law.

Bob smiled. He knew her happiness was less about seeing

16

Jim and Karen than in avoiding the question. He fooled around and so did she. Nothing new about that. They'd been doing it for most of their marriage. They just didn't talk about it that often. They weren't swingers, after all.

Jim noted the glasses in his parents' hands. His mother was closest, so he spoke to her. "Drinking, Mom?"

"Yes. Want one?"

Jim frowned. "You shouldn't drink. Neither should you, Dad."

"Nothing wrong with a drink now and then, Jim," Bob replied. Especially when you're around.

"You're not getting any younger, Dad. You need to take care of your health, and drinking isn't good for you."

Bob took another sip. "It is, actually. Just so you don't drink too much."

Susan motioned for Karen to sit on the sofa.

"The best way to avoid giving in to temptation," Jim said, "is to avoid the temptation."

"Or you can just give in and enjoy yourself," Bob laughed. "Life is short, Jim. Death is forever. Enjoy life while you have the chance."

"Eternity is forever, Dad," Jim said, his voice automatically slipping into a pulpit cadence. "But it's up to you what it will be like. Will you dwell in eternal bliss in heaven, surrounded by everyone who ever meant anything to you? Or do you spend eternity burning in hell? It's up to you, you know."

Bob started walking back to his chair. "I really don't worry about it." He sat down, sipped at his drink. This visit was starting out like most, and he suspected he'd be fairly well sotted before the day was over. "And you're not on television now. You're here to help us celebrate our anniversary, so be joyful, why don't you?"

"Right," Susan chimed in. "Have a good time. If you don't want a drink, we have iced tea or pop in the refrigerator. Karen?"

"Iced tea would be fine, Mom," she said, very softly.

"Jim?"

"You have Coke?"

"Sure."

"Okay, then Coke."

Susan placed her drink on the table behind the sofa and went out through the dining room archway.

Bob settled back in his chair. Time to be civil, he thought. Perhaps this time it might even be reciprocated. "How was your trip?"

Jim was sitting on the love seat at the far side of the room. "It was okay. The airlines just aren't what they used to be. Not even flying first class. Lousy food, plastic forks. It's like what you used to get in tourist. For what it costs to fly first class we should be treated better."

Bob glanced over at Karen. She didn't appear to be at all interested in Jim's description of their flight from Dallas. Well, she rarely said anything. She just sat there, looking proper, while her husband complained about being treated like everyone else. He preached equality, but, like Orwell's pigs, some were obviously a little more equal than others.

"How about your rental car?" Bob asked. "Are you happy with that?"

"That was fine."

"What did you get?"

"Caddy SUV. We picked it up at Hopkins and drove down. Took about two hours."

"Why Cleveland? You could have flown into Columbus and been here in under an hour."

Jim shrugged. "No direct flights. We'd have spent more time waiting around in Chicago to make the connection than it took to drive here from Cleveland."

Bob nodded. He couldn't fault his son on that. He didn't care for hanging about airports himself.

Susan returned from the kitchen, carrying two glasses. She gave one to Karen, then walked over to Jim and gave him the other. Karen merely said "Thanks," and Jim had an odd look on his face. Karen was the only one who recognized that look. It didn't make her feel good. Jim would naturally have expected to be served first, which he would have been had he been sitting on the sofa and Karen on the love seat. Susan had served Karen first because she had to walk past her to get to her son. Jim's priorities were always men first.

Susan, oblivious to this breach of what was, after all, merely Jim's personal version of etiquette, picked up her own drink from the table and plopped into her chair next to her husband.

Jim decided to let it pass for the moment. "So," he said, "you two have been married for 40 years now. How'd you do it? Any secrets to reveal?"

Susan shook her head. "We're used to each other."

Bob nodded. "I expect that's the actual secret. It just wouldn't seem normal not to have the other around."

"No matter how annoying he is," Susan added.

Bob looked at his wife, smiled, and lifted his glass to his lips.

Looking around, Jim noticed the stack of books on the table behind the sofa. That reminded him of something. "One of my vestrymen was talking to me about your latest book a few days ago," he said, rising. "You do know we're going to do whatever we can to make sure it isn't sold in our town. What if some innocent child reads it?"

Bob pushed himself up out of his chair. "If a child can understand it, I suppose it might do him some good."

"Dad, you're saying that God is a myth. Everyone knows that isn't true."

"Everyone doesn't. But I suppose you have to act like he's real or people will stop giving you money, won't they?"

Jim looked at his father the way someone might look at a particularly dense child. How could someone with an Oxford DPhil, and a near genius IQ, fail to see the obvious? "There's more to it than money. Money is the least of it. There are souls to be saved. I want people to come to Jesus so that they can go to heaven when they die. It really bothers me that you're almost certainly going to hell if you don't change your ways."

"No such place, Jim. You exist only in your body—in your brain, really—and when you die, and your brain dies, that's the end of you. No afterlife; just total oblivion. Nor will you care. You won't be there to experience it."

Time to change the subject, Susan thought. "Are you two getting into it again?"

"It passes the time," Bob replied. For him, that's all it was. He found overtly religious people amusing, as well as a little sad. They were missing out on so much in life.

"Well, there has to be a better way to do that," Susan said. She turned to her daughter-in-law. "Karen, what about you? Still not pregnant again?" The one thing Susan still wanted in life were a few grandchildren to spoil. So far that hadn't worked out.

"I'm afraid not," Karen said.

Jim sat on the sofa next to his wife, taking her hand. "The Lord hasn't blessed us with another baby yet, Mom. But we're working on it."

"How long has it been?" Bob asked, returning to his chair.

"Six years," James answered. "Six years since Morgan died, and we're still waiting for another. I don't know why we haven't had another yet, but God will provide when he sees fit, right?"

Bob took another drink. "You never paid attention in biology, did you?"

Jim returned a look that somehow managed to combine annoyance with embarrassment. He hated it when a discussion started to edge toward sex. "I know how it works, Dad. It just hasn't happened yet."

"I'm sure it will," Susan offered.

"God will provide," Jim stated.

"Right." Bob shrugged, deciding it was time to change the subject. He didn't care about his son, but Karen was looking decidedly uncomfortable. "You know," he said, "I got the retirement letter at my office today."

"From the college?" Susan asked. "Or just the usual nagging letter from the AARP?"

"From the college."

"Are you retiring?" Jim asked. He could get into this topic. It was one where there wasn't much reason to argue.

"I hope to eventually. I'm not planning to go like Professor Holden, dropping dead in the middle of a lecture."

"Aren't you a little young to retire?"

"I'm 64, which is presumably why I received the letter. It's just an offer, not a mandate. I can just keep working if I want to."

"Do you?"

"I haven't decided." Bob was about to say more, but stopped at the sound of car doors closing. Good, he thought, that should be one of the normal kids.

VI

EVERYONE GOT TO THEIR FEET AS THE FRONT DOOR opened. Bob smiled broadly as his daughter Ellen, and her husband Mark, came in. She was their youngest, and had always been his favorite. Ellen took after her mother in some ways. Both of them were short, and their personalities were similar. But Susan had dark brown hair—kept that way with a little help from her hairdresser—which she kept fairly short, while her daughter's hair was red and worn long.

Today Ellen was wearing a simple green dress. Mark, who generally looked like a construction worker, but was actually an obstetrician, wore jeans, a long sleeved denim shirt with the cuffs turned up, and beat up tennis shoes. More often than not Ellen left him behind in Canton when she came to visit. There was usually someone having a baby, and delivering them took priority over seeing the in-laws. Today was special, though. For her parents' anniversary he could damn well push all the work off onto his partner.

After the usual hugs, Ellen headed straight for the bar. Mark sat on the love seat.

"I thought we'd never get here," she said, building a couple of drinks. She could see that her brother was annoyed by this, but really didn't care. Her brother, she thought, was a nut.

"What happened?" Susan asked.

Mark spoke up. "There was an accident on 30, a few miles west of 250. Somebody turned over a semi and completely blocked the westbound lanes."

"It took them nearly an hour to get a detour set up," Ellen said, still working on the drinks. "Then we had to turn around and go back to 250. No one was going to be getting through on 30 for a while."

"So then we took 250 over to 71," Mark continued. "Well, by the time you're to 71, you're nearly in Ashland."

"Sounds like an adventure," Bob said. "Think how boring life would be if everything always went as expected."

Ellen finished mixing the drinks and carried them over to the love seat, giving one to Mark. "Nothing wrong with boring, Dad.

Bob shrugged. "Nothing particularly good about it, either." As far as Bob was concerned, life was supposed to be an adventure. To his way of thinking, you got one chance at it, and then you were gone, so why not enjoy it while you were here?

"Did you guys know Dad was thinking of retiring?" Jim offered.

Ellen looked at her father. "Are you?"

"Not very seriously, but the opportunity has been offered."

"We're not really that old yet," Susan added.

"What do you mean, offered?" Ellen asked.

"I was 64 on my last birthday. That's when the college makes the offer. It's just standard procedure."

"Would you do it?"

"Possibly. Your mum would have a lot to say on that, mind."

Susan sat forward in her chair. "Damn right. I won't be eligible for another seven years. Can you imagine this old fart waiting around the house for me to retire? It would drive him nuts." She thought for a moment. "Wouldn't do much for *my* sanity, either."

"When I retire," Bob said, "I think I want to travel. Perhaps buy one of those big caravans and drive all over the country. Not that easy to do if your wife is still teaching full time."

"It would get him out of the house, though. And out of my hair."

"You'd soon grow lonely, and so would I."

"I'd just find some nice freshman who had the hots for a sexy, older English Lit professor."

"Mom!" Jim half rose from the sofa, then sat back down. "You shouldn't even joke about stuff like that!"

Susan swallowed a bit more of her drink. "Who says I'm joking?"

Bob nodded. "I believe her. And just what makes you think I'd be travelling alone?"

Jim shook his head. Not *his* parents, he thought. His father was an idol worshipping atheist—Jim honestly couldn't see why that wasn't possible, because obviously everyone had to worship *something*, didn't they?—but he'd never known any two people who were more obviously still in love with each other even after 40 years of marriage. "You two have been married too long. You'll stay together."

"Yeah," Ellen said. "I just can't imagine the two of you apart."

Bob smiled wickedly. "I can." That reverie was ended by the sound of his wife's hand slapping down on the little table between their chairs. "But then I think about it and decide that I wouldn't care for it very much."

"See," Jim said.

"So," Ellen said, "you're *not* going to retire."

"Probably not."

"The longer we work," Susan explained, "the bigger the pension checks will be when we finally do retire. Extra money will always come in handy."

"Money shouldn't be the only concern, though," Jim noted.

Ellen frowned at her big brother. "Easy for you to say. You're rich."

"I'm not rich. Your salary is probably bigger than mine."

"Jim, you drive a Bentley. Your car's worth more than our house." Ellen taught third grade, and had completed her masters a year ago. Between what she made, and Mark's income from his practice, they were quite comfortable. But there was no way they'd even think about spending a quarter million dollars for a car.

"It's not my car," Jim explained. "It belongs to the church. I just get to drive it."

Susan glanced over at Bob. She knew where that sort of statement was likely to lead. Time to change the subject again, and she knew just where to lead it.

"So, Ellen—any news on the baby front over there in Canton?"

"Nothing yet, Mom."

Too late. "That's just how it works with the big churches, isn't it, Jim?" Bob interjected. "Put everything in the church's name and avoid the taxes."

"The ability to tax is the ability to control." It was a cliche, Jim knew, but that didn't mean it wasn't true.

"There's a difference between taxing church real estate and taxing church income. A business is a business. We'd go a long way towards eliminating the deficit if churches had to pay income taxes."

"Dad, why do you keep trying to make God mad at you."

Bob shook his head sadly. "I don't. I can't imagine why I'd want to. What's your imaginary friend going to do to me, do you think?"

Why does he do this, Jim wondered. It was so obvious that everything in the Bible was true. People wouldn't have believed it for so many centuries otherwise. People only believed true things in the long run. Besides, he knew what he felt when he read the Bible, and he knew what he felt when he prayed. It couldn't just be psychology. He wasn't just talking himself into belief. You couldn't really do that, he was sure.

"God is real, Dad. And it really bothers me that you seem sure to find out only after it's too late."

"Oh, will you two behave yourselves?" Susan half rose from her chair. "Jim, you're not going to save your father. And Bob, you're not going to change Jim's beliefs."

Bob grunted and swallowed more of his drink. I should be drinking the blended stuff, he thought. Such a waste of a good single malt, angry drinking. "I'd be happy," he said, "if he'd just develop some critical thinking skills."

"Ultimately," Jim declared, "you just have to go with what God said. He made us, he made the world we live in and gave it to us, so he gets to set the rules."

"Which god did this?"

"There's only one, Dad."

"Actually, there are something like 30,000 of them. And how do you know you've picked the right one? How do you know that everything you say in that big church of yours, or on your television show, isn't just digging you into a deeper hole with Zeus? And one bright, sunny afternoon he'll have had enough and shove a lightning bolt up your arse?"

"There's only one God, Dad," Jim said. "Mine. I know that for a fact."

"There are no gods, Jim. Instead of trying to ban my latest book, you should try reading it. You might learn something."

Every time, Susan thought. This happens every time those two get together. She looked at Karen, who was sitting very still, looking straight ahead. Susan had never seen anyone look quite so calm. How could she do that? Didn't it bother her to see her husband arguing with his father?

Meditation of some sort? Well, prayer, probably. Karen was just as religious as her husband. That was obvious when you saw her on his TV program.

She looked at her daughter, who was now sitting on the arm of the sofa, only a couple feet away, looking decidedly uncomfortable, though not as uncomfortable as Mark, who looked as if he'd like nothing better than to hop in the car and head back to Canton.

"Maybe," Susan told Ellen, "you should try harder. You *want* kids, right? I'm sure you can get pregnant if you just try hard enough. That's how *you* got here."

"We're already going at it like minks, Mom. It just isn't happening."

"Do we really need to go into details, Hun?"

Mark looked more than a little embarrassed to hear his sex life being discussed by his wife and mother-in-law. How in the world, Susan wondered, did listening to a couple of women talk about sex manage to embarrass a gynecologist?

"If we want these two to stop fussing at each other," Susan said, walking to the middle of the room and getting between her husband and son, "I think we do, yes."

"No."

Susan looked at Jim, while pushing Bob back toward his chair. "No?"

"No," Jim repeated, sitting beside his wife. "You don't need to go into detail. Sex is something that should be kept very private. What happens in the bedroom is something that's between a man and his wife, and no one else needs to know anything about it."

Karen glanced at her husband. No, you wouldn't want anyone to know, would you? She turned her attention back to the squirrel that was trying very hard to climb the greased pole holding up a bird feeder on the front lawn. Stay out of this, she told herself.

"We've been thinking about *in vitro*," Ellen said. "My doctor thinks it might be our best hope."

"Ellen, you can't do that," Jim declared. "It's wrong."

Mark looked at his brother-in-law with, perhaps, less surprise than he would have with anyone else. His wife's doctor was Fred Collins, Mark's partner. The poor guy was stuck back in Canton this weekend and probably going to have to deliver Mrs Etling's third kid before it was over.

"What are you talking about?" Mark asked. "I've got several patients we've done that for. It's a common procedure."

"Then you should know how it works. They create a lot more embryos than they implant. Sure, they store the extras for a while, but eventually they just murder them."

Bob slumped back in his chair. "I wish we'd made you go to a real college. Then maybe you'd know the difference between biology and mythology."

"Dad, you call yourself a Republican, but you sure don't sound like one."

"Of course I sound like one. I'm a traditional Republican. There may be as many as 300 of us left in the country." What those idiots running the party today were, he had no bloody idea, but they were certainly not Republicans. Not as Lincoln, or Roosevelt, or Eisenhower, or Rockefeller saw the party, at least. Conservative fiscally, liberal socially, that was how it was supposed to be. The current lot would probably fight to *keep* slavery. He frowned to himself. Some of them were; they called it being "pro-life," but it was still slavery.

VII

GEORGE ANDERSON COULD HEAR THE SHOUTING FROM the front porch. He looked at Eric Simpson, who was, as usual, looking a bit nervous. Well, Eric was only really outgoing in court, wasn't he? Otherwise he was very shy and soft spoken.

"They sound angry," Eric said.

"That's my dad and my brother. They always yell at each other. Doesn't mean they don't love each other. But, well, my brother Jim is kind of a dick."

"The TV evangelist guy?"

"Right."

"They're all dicks. I think there's a law that they have to be."

"You could be right," George agreed. "Come on, let's go in."

He opened the door, pleased to notice that his entrance was greeted with a sudden silence. His mother rushed over to the door and hugged him.

"George! You made it!"

"Hi, Mom. Dad. Guys." He hurried into the room, hugging his father, who responded rather warmly for an Englishman. Well, his dad never had been one to confirm the cliches, except maybe for how he dressed. He nodded to Karen, walked right past his brother, hugged his sister, and shook hands with Mark. It was good to be home.

"Shortest distance to travel," Bob commented dryly. "So naturally you're the last to get here."

"I know how long it takes to get here, Dad. And you said by two, so we're still early."

Bob tugged out his watch. It was five minutes till. "I suppose. But you could have been earlier." *And then maybe I could have avoided arguing with your idiot brother.*

"Well, we're here now. And why are you being so grouchy? You been talking to Jim again?"

"And, as usual, always on the wrong subjects," Susan said. She looked over by the door, where Eric was standing with a sheepish look on his face. "Who's your friend?"

"Oh, this is Eric Simpson, my roommate."

"Hi," Eric said, tentatively.

George pulled Eric into the room and started pointing. "That's my sister Ellen over there," he said, "with her husband, Mark. He's a doctor. The sourpuss in the overpriced suit is my brother Jim, and that's his wife, Karen, with him. And, of course, Mom and Dad. Dad is Bob, Mom is Sue, or if you can't remember their names, just call either of them 'Doc.' They're both PhDs, and they both teach here. Dad teaches philosophy, Mom teaches English Lit."

"Nice to meet you, Eric," Susan said. "Why don't you two get yourselves something to drink."

"Good idea, Mom."

George led Eric toward the bar, but indicated for him to sit down as they were passing the love seat. Eric looked over at Ellen, who was sitting on the love seat's arm close to the bar. "You know," he said softly, "your dad dresses like the Doctor, doesn't he?"

Ellen smiled, looking across the room at her father. *Serves you right for wearing the burgundy tie today,* she thought. It was an old joke in the family by now, except for Jim, who only watched religious programming and had never seen Matt Smith's Doctor. Or any of the others, for that matter.

"No," Bob grunted, "the Doctor dresses like me. I was

dressing like this back when Hartnell was still trying to keep his grand-daughter's teachers out of the Tardis."

Eric looked at him curiously. Eric's familiarity with the show had begun with Christopher Eccleston, and he was now quite sure that his lame joke wasn't going to work very well with this British sounding college professor who obviously knew the older shows as well.

Bob knew the older shows *very* well. He had watched the second broadcast of the pilot in 1963 on the BBC on his parents' television. They'd missed the first, as had most people, with everyone watching coverage of the Kennedy assassination instead.

"At least," Bob continued, "this is how I dressed when I was home from school. At school we wore uniform."

"What school was that?" Eric asked, already figuring he wouldn't really recognize the answer. It just seemed polite to ask.

"Eton. Then Oxford. With nine months of military service in between." A training accident had put paid to any thoughts of an Army career, though it didn't inconvenience him that much after all these years.

Oh. Eric had heard of both of those. "So," he said, "you come from a rich family? I mean, aren't those upper class schools?"

"We certainly weren't rich by the time I came along," Bob said. "Death duties, you see. We'd had money once, but the government gets to take a substantial piece of it every time someone dies. Also, I'm the third of four sons, and *primogenitor* still applies. My eldest brother gets the house, the land, what's left of the money, and the title. All I got out of it was a good education."

"Title?"

"My father is the current Lord Anderson of North Barrow."

Eric was impressed. "Now that's kind of cool. But you don't have a title?"

"Only the academic one."

"So just what *is* a lord, anyway?"

"Well, my father is a baron. Generally, if someone is just called Lord So-and-so, he's a baron. The higher grades are usually referred to by their titles. In my family's case, my fourth great-grandfather was a general who was ennobled by George III during the Seven Years War." He thought a moment. "Here they call it the French and Indian Wars."

Eric shrugged and shook his head. "I guess I didn't pay that much attention in history class."

"Before the American Revolution. George Washington was fighting on the British side in that one." And that, Bob thought, was it for the history lessons. Let the young man go look on the Internet if he wanted to learn more. Or read a book.

Jim leaned forward. "Did you know Dad was thinking of retiring."

George handed Eric a drink and sat down beside him. "That's cool, Dad. Give you some time to relax."

"I'm not retiring. Not yet."

"We've talked about it," Susan said. "But I don't think we'll do it until I'm eligible too. So it won't be for a few years yet. Then we get the motor home."

"Motor home?" George found he was having a little trouble imagining his slightly uptight parents in a motor home.

"We'd both like the travel," Bob said. "With a big caravan…"

"Wait," George said, unable to resist. "You mean one of those big, boxy looking things? Blue, maybe?"

I'm not going to dignify that with an answer. "…we could follow the seasons. Go where it's warm in the winter, maybe go north to where it's cooler in the summer."

"Yes," Susan agreed. "Warm winters would be very nice."

"Come on down to Texas," Jim said. "We get you going to church every Sunday there's a chance we can save you yet."

"From what?"

Hoping to forestall further argument, Susan spoke up. "George, get them onto a different subject, will you? They get into this same argument every time Jim is here, and it's not getting anyone anywhere."

George looked at Eric, then back at his mother. Was it time yet? Probably not. "I do have something to say that would probably stop this argument, but I'm afraid it'll just start another one."

"Couldn't you just talk about football or something?"

Bob laughed. "Jim would just try to claim the Cowboys are better than the Browns and start a different sort of religious war."

Jim looked slightly puzzled. Growing up near Columbus, he hadn't really formed any strong attachment to either of the Ohio professional teams. But he lived in the Dallas suburbs, and his church provided him with season tickets. "The Cowboys *are* better," he stated.

Eric looked at George. "Your dad likes football?" He figured the British accent would translate to a preference for British sports, and the American version of football wasn't something he thought of being in that category.

"Oh, I do indeed," Bob said. "Though, all in all, I much prefer baseball."

"Texas Rangers," Jim said. He had home game tickets to those as well.

"Cleveland Indians," Bob asserted.

Here they go again, Susan thought. "So, Eric, what do you do for a living."

"I'm a lawyer. Family law, mostly."

"Family law," Bob mused. "That would be divorces, no?"

"Mostly. But wills, custody, trusts, adoptions, child support, anything along those lines. That's actually how I met George. There was a business in an estate and we needed a CPA to audit the books."

George nodded, looking amused. "Yeah, and was that business ever screwed up. I think it took about four weeks to get it all sorted out."

"Worth it, though," Eric offered.

"So, where do you go to church, Eric?" Jim asked.

Eric looked at him. Why the hell should you care? "I grew up in a Nazarene church. Haven't been much lately. After a while you get tired of listening to all the hellfire and brimstone preaching."

Jim smiled. "It's good for you. Reminds you of what's important."

"Mostly, I just got the impression the preacher was obsessed with sex. Or he was afraid people might be having it. Something like that."

"As long as you're married, sex is fine," Jim said. "If you're not, well, obviously you can't have sex."

"My mother used to think that way," Eric grunted. "My sister asked her once if you could have a baby if you weren't married and my mom said you couldn't. My sister was *not* happy when she found out you *could*. It just never occurred to her that what mom really meant was you weren't supposed to, not that there was some magical thing that would keep a single girl from getting knocked up."

"I was still a virgin when I got married," Ellen chimed in.

"Really?" George found this fascinating, along with unlikely. "You stayed a virgin until you were 27?"

"Yes, I did."

"Why?" Bob asked, which wasn't exactly the response Ellen had expected from her father. "I applaud the dedication, of course, but why?"

Ellen laughed softly. Jim's expression was priceless. He couldn't seem to decide whether he was supposed to be pleased to hear she had resisted the Satanic call of illicit sex before marriage, or appalled that their father seemed to think there was something strange about the whole idea of premarital celibacy.

"Well," she said, "it wasn't because I was afraid I'd get punished or anything. I mean, obviously no one is really going to hell for screwing around. I think I was mostly just afraid I'd get knocked up, or maybe catch something."

George was leaning back on the love seat, laughing. "Hell, I barely made it into junior high."

"It's different for boys," Ellen said. "You can't get pregnant."

"We can still catch things. There are worse things than getting pregnant, you know."

Ellen was starting to feel her drink. She was barely over five feet tall, and weighed only 102 pounds. She'd never be able to drink all that much. She just didn't have the body mass to absorb the alcohol. By now she was just tipsy enough to be getting playful.

"What about you, Jim? How long did you last?"

"Is this anything to be talking about?"

George moved over to the couch, practically leaning over his older brother. "Yes, I think it is. When did you lose your virginity, big brother?"

Such a ridiculous question, Jim thought. There could really only be one possible answer. "On the night I got married, obviously. You know what happens to fornicators. It's better to marry than to burn."

Bob laughed. "I'm fairly sure Paul meant to burn with *desire*, not in hell."

Jim glared at his father. He hated nothing quite as much as when the old man instantly identified his Bible references and then tried to use them against him. It just seemed wrong when an atheist knew the Bible better than most Christians. It was even more annoying when he was forced to admit that this was a general truism, and not just the consequences of being raised by a philosophy professor.

Then again, it might not be such a bad thing. Most Christians didn't have the scriptural sophistication to understand the subtleties, so it was better if you just gave them the right passages and explained how things worked.

"Impure desires will lead you to hell, though," he said. "And, George, what would have happened if you'd got some poor girl pregnant? How would that have looked."

"Oh, there was never any danger of that."

Bob leaned toward his wife. "I don't suppose there was, was there?"

Susan smiled. Not with George, she thought.

"There's always a risk of that," Jim insisted.

George studied his brother. Jim, he thought, you may be the most unobservant human being who ever lived. His parents had obviously caught the implication. Jim was just oblivious. Or perhaps he simply refused to see what was right in front of him.

Well, Jim was a jerk. He always had been. George couldn't see that becoming a minister had changed that.

Still, it was probably now or never. His family needed to know what was happening. Better now than finding out later by accident.

"I suppose I should tell you my news," he said.

"Good news?" his mother asked.

"I think so. Jimmy here will probably have a stroke when he hears it."

Jim looked at him curiously.

"So what is it?" Susan asked. "Are you finally settling down?"

"Well, so much for surprising you guys."

"You're getting married?" Jim asked.

"That's the idea."

"So, who's the lucky girl."

Right, George thought. Oblivious idiot.

"I suppose I am," Eric said.

"What???!!!!"

"Eric and I are getting married."

"To each other?" Jim was sputtering badly now. He'd just be presented with an impossible situation.

"Of course."

"But, you can't. It's illegal. You can't do that."

"We're moving to New York," George informed him. "It's legal there."

"Oh, I know that. I also know that just about as soon as they made it legal, God shoved a hurricane right up lower Manhattan."

Bob put his drink on the table. "Is is being on television that makes so many preachers think that way? Looking for ratings? Why are you blaming a natural disaster on something the voters did?"

Silly question. He knew why, because the Bible was written in a time when people couldn't explain much of anything that happened in nature, so they assigned everything to a god. Science had explained what caused storms long ago, even if it wasn't yet that good at predicting exactly what they'd do, but people still clung to their supernatural explanations.

"You two can't get married," James ranted on. "It's perverted. It's unnatural. It's an abomination. If you give in to these perverted lusts, you'll spend all eternity burning in hell!"

George snorted and walked to the bar. "Oh, grow up."

"This is what's causing most of the trouble for this country. If we could only get rid of all the fornicators and sodomites Jesus would come back and all our problems would be over."

Karen shook her head. This was getting to be too much even for her. She didn't really have a family, except for these people, and she hated the idea of potentially driving one of them away. She liked George. He was always nice to her.

"Jim, he's your brother."

"You be quiet."

"Sorry."

Bob thought she looked afraid as she apologized for speaking up. A damned silly thing to apologize for, come to that.

"You know," Eric said, joining George at the bar, "your brother seemed like a fairly nice person when we first got here."

George handed him a fresh drink. "He can give that impression. But he's really a sort of hyper-religious asshole. I warned you to watch a few hours of his show. He goes off like this during most of them, trying to blame everything that's wrong with the world on people like us."

They all do that, Eric thought.

"No, really," Jim went on, "just when did you decide to turn into a queer, George?"

George grabbed Eric's arm, snickering. "He said 'decide'."

"So does that mean he thinks there's a choice involved?"

"Probably."

"Of course there's a choice," Jim exploded. "There's always a choice. God lets you decide whether you'll obey his laws, or just give in to your lusts."

"No, Jim, there's no choice," George said, trying to stay calm. Had there been? he wondered. Had there ever a time when he could have convinced himself that he liked women instead of men? No, he decided, there hadn't. "I've been gay for as long as I can remember, and I'm fairly sure I was gay even before that and just didn't know what to call it."

Eric poked his elbow into Jim's arm. "Still," he said, "it's nice of you to admit to being bisexual."

Jim turned, looking for a moment as if he might strike Eric, but then seemed to think better of it. Eric was a couple inches shorter, but had the hard look of a seasoned athlete. Or of someone who spent a lot of time in a gym. While Jim looked fit and trim, he knew perfectly well that much of his own athletic look came from careful tailoring, not exercise. Still, deciding that Eric could almost certainly clean up the floor with him if anything became physical didn't reduce his anger in the slightest.

"What the hell are you talking about," Jim shouted. "I'm not some sort of pervert."

I never said you were, moron. "Are you sure of that?" Eric asked. It would like explaining things to a child. Not a particularly bright child, either. "How can you think there's a choice unless you *have* a choice? You only have a choice if you're bisexual, so logically you must *be* bisexual." He smiled. "I know I never had a choice about it."

"That's right," George said.

"Damned perverts. Don't try that sort of shit with me."

"Jim, watch your language!" Susan decided it was time to remind him just where he was. To remind all of them, really, but especially Jim. "Disagree all you want, but don't swear in my house."

Bob got up and started walking back to the bar. He paused at the end of the sofa. "And try to have a little more respect for your wife, too. Her opinion holds just as much weight as yours. And she's right—he *is* your brother."

Bob touched her on the shoulder as he finished. It was meant to be reassuring, but she flinched, almost imperceptibly, as if it were anything but. What was that about? he wondered.

"Thank you," she said, her voice very subdued.

Bob continued to the bar and made another drink. This time he poured the blended Scotch. This seemed likely to be one of those days when he was just going to get drunk and be damned with it. The cheap stuff really was good enough for that.

"This is what happens when you grow up without God in your life, Dad," Jim declaimed. He had a tendency to sound like he was in the pulpit whenever he wanted to make a point. "Granddad failed you very badly when he didn't give you a proper religious education."

He taught me everything anyone really needed to know about it, Bob thought. He taught me how to think for myself.

"The Bible is the word of God, and the Bible says that the man is the head of the house and the master over his wife. Karen will do as she's told, because that's the way God wants it."

"You did *not* learn that nonsense from me."

"It's not nonsense, it's the word of God! I may not have learned it from you, but it was always there for me to learn. Most of my high school friends came from good Christian homes. We'd talk. I learned about the Bible, what God wanted, and how Jesus gave us a way out of sin and into heaven."

Bob sipped at his drink, shaking his head. "Have you ever actually read the Bible?" he asked.

"Of course I've read the Bible." His inflection made it clear he considered this a particularly silly question.

"All of it? Starting at the beginning and reading straight through?" Bob felt sure he hadn't. Nearly everyone read it in bits and pieces, skipping over the boring parts, or whatever they didn't really agree with.

"Will you two knock it off?" Susan was between them now, and not looking at all happy. This was supposed to be a happy occasion. She was sure of that.

"Sorry," Bob said. "I just find it hard to put up with his lack of tolerance."

George looked up from the sofa. "He was just like this in high school." He thought for a moment. "Well, not with me, but that's only because he thought I was straight. And certainly not around you two. Being a bigot doesn't make you stupid about everything. But to anyone he thought might be gay he was an asshole." He smiled. "And that included several straight kids."

"I never saw any of that," Bob said, wondering if he should have.

"He knew enough to keep it quiet at home."

"Well, I knew you were gay."

"You did? You never said anything."

"I presumed you knew. And that you'd get around to telling us when the time was right."

"Yeah, it was always pretty obvious," Ellen interjected.

Apparently not to Jim, George thought.

Susan sat on the arm of the sofa, looking over at George and Eric. "So," she said, "when's the wedding?"

George looked at Eric, shrugging slightly, then back at his mother. "Next year, probably. We have to move first, and that's going to be a bit of a hassle. Another set of CPA and bar exams to take, so that we'll be able to work in New York."

"Easier for you, though," Eric said. "You can get a damn good job even before you get the New York certification. I'm a little old to be clerking while I wait for admission."

"You'll probably pass on your first try," George said.

"So just how does this wedding thing work, anyway?" Bob asked. Who gets walked down the aisle and given to whom? Or does anyone?"

George looked up. "I hadn't really thought about it. I suppose nobody. It's not like one of us will be wearing a wedding gown, is it?"

"Why not?" Jim snorted. "Don't fags like to dress up like women?"

"Most cross dressers are straight, actually," Eric said.

"Men shouldn't wear dresses, and women shouldn't wear men's clothes. Period." Jim was now sounding very much like he was preaching. "And, Dad, what's the matter with you?"

"Oh, any number of things. But I suppose you have something particular in mind?"

"You're telling George it's okay to be a fag. Do you really want your son to go to hell when he dies?"

Bob took a very large swallow of his drink. Jim thought of himself as a success, but Bob could only think of him as a massive failure of his own parenting skills. He should have been able to make a better man of him.

"You always seemed very intelligent as a child. I suppose you can quote most of the Bible from memory by now. But you never learned to think for yourself. You just never learned that you should question things when they make no rational sense."

"God was very explicit on this subject," Jim declared. "Sleeping with another man is an abomination, and we're supposed to kill anyone who does."

"Is that what it says?" his father asked.

"Of course it is."

41

"Well then, let me quote it for you. *'If a man also lie with mankind, as he lieth with a woman, both of them have committed an abomination; they shall surely be put to death; their blood shall be upon them.'* That's the passage you're talking about, right?

"Right. It's all very clear."

"You think so? I find two rather obvious issues with this. First, my friend Rabbi Lehrman tells me that the word translated as abomination *always* refers to some act of idol worship. So the reference is almost certainly to some ancient Canaanite cult practice, and not to personal relationships. Secondly, the last time I looked, it wasn't actually possible for a man to lie with a man in the same way he'd lie with a woman. I've never met a man with a vagina, have you?"

It's like talking to a child, Jim thought. "You're being too literal."

"Oh, I don't know. Maybe God only wants people to have anal sex." Or maybe, he thought, whoever really wrote that particular passage was both thoroughly closeted and pathologically celibate and just didn't know any better. Or, being Jewish, had merely taken the historical Jewish attitude that harsh laws should be looked upon as a challenge as to why they shouldn't ever be applied literally. Biblical law seemed to imply that in some cases mutilation was approved of—an eye for an eye, and the like—but Jews had always figured what God had in mind there was tort law, since literal physical equivalence wasn't possible, if you caused someone to lose an eye you'd have to pay him its value.

"It's just wrong, Dad. God said to kill queers, not let them marry each other."

"And you've never wondered about that?"

"About what?"

"Why doesn't God just kill them himself? He's supposed to be omnipotent, right? So why does he always seem to need a pack of homicidal fanatics to do his killing for him? For that matter, if he's really omnipotent, why doesn't he just make everyone straight?"

Jim shook his head sadly. "Dad, you really need to learn to

see the truth. God is real, and he's set out the ways we need to act, to behave, if we're going to have eternal life in heaven."

"I know," Bob sighed. "He threatens to torture people forever because he loves them." Though not, he thought, apparently as much as he did before Jesus, since until then the worst thing he'd do was kill you and be done with it, but after he added eternal punishment and torture. Apparently Christians needed a little more threatening to keep them in line. Well, the early ones were mostly former pagans; they were used to their gods being jerks.

"You might want to think about something, Jim. Do you really want your brother mad at you for the rest of your life? What if you need him some day? Need his help, I mean?"

"It's not me, Dad, it's what God said."

Bob swallowed the last of his drink and walked over to the bar for a refill. Be calm, he thought. Jim can't seem to help being a monomaniacal idiot.

"So God," he said, "who already knows exactly how they'll respond, tests people anyway, knowing they'll fail? And then punishes them forever when they do? Are you claiming that God is some sort of cosmic sadist? That he enjoys sending most of humanity to hell?"

"People make their own decisions," Ellen interjected.

Bob slopped a little more Scotch into his glass. "Are you taking Jim's side in this?"

Ellen shook her head. "No, not really." She looked over at George. "I think it takes a lot of guts to do what George is doing, considering the state of the world. But people do still make their own decisions."

"You really think so?"

"Sure."

"What if everyone *really* thought for themselves?" He was on comfortable ground here, back to being the philosophy professor. "What if everyone decided what was best based on objective reality? How well would Jim's Bible stories hold up then?"

"You are my father," Jim declaimed. "George is my brother. What sort of son or brother would I be if I didn't do whatever I could to keep the two of you from going to hell? God tests everyone, and you'd better be sure you pass the test."

"You're not saving anyone from anything," George asserted. "I'm gay. Live with it."

"How can you be gay? You were captain of the high school football team! You dated cheerleaders!"

"Suzi Decker," George said. "We always double dated with Jerry Fitzpatrick and Jeannie Loman." He nudged Eric. "It was always the same two couples. It's just that Jim here is still a little confused as to who the couples actually were."

"Pervert!"

"Jim!" Karen blurted it out, instantly knowing she shouldn't have. There would be repercussions.

"Shut up, Karen," Jim growled. "Speak when you're spoken to."

"Jim!" Susan's tone of voice left no doubt she didn't approve any more than Karen. It also left no doubt that he'd damn well better not answer back.

Bob took another large swallow of Scotch and headed for the front door. "I need some air," he said, going out onto the front porch.

"So do I," Susan declared, giving Jim a particularly annoyed look. Some anniversary.

VIII

BOB ANDERSON STOOD BY THE PORCH RAILING, LOOKING out over the front lawn. The squirrel was still trying to climb the greased pipe that supported the bird feeder. He had to give the little creature marks for persistence.

Three cars were parked on the side lawn, just off the driveway, where they wouldn't block each other in. Jim's big rented Caddy SUV was closest to the house. Then Mark and Ellen's dark gray Accura sedan, perhaps a modern version of the traditional doctor's Buick. Closest to the street was George's Honda Civic. It was the way he was. Despite a rather flamboyant personality—how the hell Jim had failed to notice that his brother was gay struck Bob as a ridiculous victory of prejudice over insight—George had always gone for very basic cars.

His own 30-year-old MGB was in the garage, along with Susan's big Ford sedan. Even after all these years, Bob was still unsure whether the sports car was a manifestation of some inner need to show off, or just a reinforcement of his own innate British identity. Or both.

"You okay?" Susan asked, joining him by the railing.

"When did he get like that? We've argued about theology for years, but I've never seen him get like this before."

Sometimes, Susan thought, the English Lit professor got to teach philosophy to the philosophy professor. "Maybe George and Eric are right."

"In what way?"

"Maybe Jim really *is* bisexual. They'd present a threat to him then, wouldn't they?"

Bob didn't quite get it. Supposedly everyone was somewhat sexually ambiguous, but he was personally far over on the hetero side. He couldn't really understand why gay men did what they did. He also didn't give a damn about it. "His grandfather and I are both very outspoken atheists. Hardly people an evangelist would want to claim as his immediate forbears. He certainly thinks we're annoying, but he doesn't seem to find us a threat."

"He's not worried that he'll suddenly slip and turn into an atheist, is he? He may even consider it a plus, because he can preach about how he found Jesus in spite of your misguided efforts to keep him ignorant. Christians love that sort of thing."

"They do, don't they?"

"But have you thought that perhaps George isn't the only one who finds Eric attractive?"

He hadn't, but now that his wife had brought it up... "I suppose that's possible."

"You know he thinks he's helping, right?"

"I know." He took a very large swallow of his drink. His wife, he noticed, seemed to be keeping up for the moment. "He also thinks that anyone who isn't *exactly* his sort of Christian is going to hell. That's probably 90 percent of humanity."

Susan nodded. "Probably more like 95 percent. Jim's *very* picky about who gets saved. No, he takes all of this very literally. That's his biggest problem. He's a bit like a computer's operating system."

"What do you mean?"

"All a computer can really do is tell the difference between a one and a zero. Between yes and no. It's a binary system; there's no maybe."

"And Jim doesn't do maybes?"

"No, he doesn't."

"He should consider it."

"Oh, I'm sure it makes him feel better to thinks there's always an absolute answer to every question."

"We'd all like that," Bob replied. "Of course, if there were, there wouldn't be much need for philosophy professors, would there? In philosophy you keep asking questions until you get an answer." He sipped at his drink, watching that ridiculously persistent squirrel resuming his efforts to get at the bird feeder. "And then you discover that Deep Thought was right, the answer is 42, and you have no idea what the bloody question really was."

"Jim doesn't think that way. He just believes whatever it says in the Bible."

"That should be confusing. It doesn't agree with itself all that well. There are two different creation stories, Jesus seems to have two almost completely different sets of paternal ancestors, that sort of thing. There's obviously a good deal of bad editing, but certainly no absolutes."

"For Jim, there are."

"That doesn't make them real," Bob insisted. "You know, my own feeling, reading the Old Testament, was that God seemed to be a very angry, disagreeable sort of character. Like an upset, omnipotent two-year-old."

"Really?"

"Really. How sensible is it to give people free will if, should they actually dare make use of it, you drown all but eight of them?"

Susan smiled and consumed a bit more of her drink. "That's Old Testament," she said. "Jim will tell you that the Jewish God was stern and judgmental, but Jesus has fixed all that."

"Has he? To my way of thinking, the New Testament God is, in some ways, far nastier and more vindictive than the Old. In any case, Christians really only changed those things they found inconvenient or uncomfortable. Things like circumcision, or having to keep kosher. They kept all the really nasty stuff—murdering homosexuals, burning witches, keeping slaves, or even just treating women as if they were."

"Well, they don't burn witches any more, do they?"

"That," Bob replied, "depends upon where you live. There are places in Africa today where Christians *do* still burn witches. Some American churches support missionaries in Uganda whose sole function seems to be lobbying the government to make homosexuality punishable by death. If there's no strong secular government to stop them, people will do whatever they think God wants them to do. Including murder each other."

"Is that the religion," Susan asked, "or the people?"

Good question, Bob thought. How much of the evil done in the name of religion came from the religion and how much from the people interpreting it? There was always someone to argue that such and such isn't what Christianity, or Islam, or any other religion was about, and that the perpetrator wasn't a 'true' believer. Well, someone, at some long ago time, had wrote down whatever inspired this so-called 'deviant' interpretation, so the bad guys could usually muster just as much scriptural evidence in support of their interpretation as the other side. Concentration camp guards had efficiently murdered Jews all week, then gone to church on Sunday feeling they'd been doing God's work. Hitler may not have thought very much of the Catholic Church, but he remained a member right up until the day he killed himself, which, being a mortal sin, presumably severed the relationship at last.

"It's the people, mostly," Bob decided. "But religion provides a convenient rationale for a lot of very bad behavior. I don't care for the way Jim treats his wife. Why in the world does she put up with this 'boss of the family' nonsense?"

Susan shrugged and emptied her glass. "She's young. She was barely 18 when she married Jim. She's only 26 now."

"And he's 37. But you were barely 18 when you married me, and you'd never put up with that sort of thing from, were I ever to be so foolish as to try it."

"You're not Jim. And you're only six years older than me, not eleven. You always encouraged me, supported my goals. I'm not sure I'm have got my PhD if you hadn't."

"You'd have done it without me."

"Maybe. But despite her being on TV with him just about every day, Jim still sees Karen as being just a housewife. She's decorative on his arm, but I don't think he sees her as an equal partner. She has only a high school education, and she's entirely dependent upon him for everything."

Bob shook his head. He looked over at Jim's rental car, thinking that it was a bit ostentatious for someone who liked to be thought of as a simple suburban parson, despite a church with more than 3,000 families on its rolls, and an income that almost certainly ran into the millions every year.

"She's not stupid," he said. "She's really a very smart girl. Smarter than Jim, if you want my opinion. But if Jim tells her to shut up, she does. And then she apologizes for saying anything in the first place. I'd end up sleeping on the sofa if I ever tried that with you."

Susan looked significantly at the porch swing. "If you were lucky," she said.

Bob looked down at the lonely ice cubes in his glass, then scanned the porch. "Do you think we should have put a bar out here?" he asked.

Susan smiled. "Might have been a good idea."

He dumped the ice cubes out over the railing into the shrubbery below. "Do we drink too much?" he wondered aloud.

"Jim thinks we do."

"Oh, Jim thinks one drink a year is too much. I'm serious, though. Do we drink too much."

"Sometimes you do."

"Only sometimes?"

"There are times you come to bed so drunk you can't do anything. Despite those pills you take."

"I take those for pulmonary hypertension and benign prostatic hyperplasia," he said, with every ounce of dignity he could manage. "I do *not* need them for the other. And that's just a side effect, anyway."

"That side effect is why most men take them," she said, "I kind of like it, and when you're too drunk you can't do it."

"Be that as it may, the question remains, do we drink too much. Specifically, do we drink too much when Jim is here?"

"Oh, when Jim is here, I don't think we drink enough."

He was much easier to take when you were thoroughly sotted, Bob thought. "How can he be so wrong about so many things, yet so bloody sure he's right?"

"You're the philosopher."

"Philosophically, I'd say we have two wonderful children—and one really annoying one.

Susan found herself giggling. "Not that bad an average for two people who only met because Ohio State let me do an exchange program at Oxford my sophomore year."

I had hair back then, Bob thought. A lot of hair. Not really long, but very thick. So thick the barber had to use thinning shears. I rather miss those days. And Susan—Susan Morton back then—young and beautiful, and brilliant into the bargain. Just turned 18, and taking her second year of college at Oxford. She was more than a little intimidating.

"Do you have any idea how scared I was back then? I very nearly didn't ask you out. I was absolutely terrified you'd say no."

"I might have. But you could have just kept asking."

"Yes, but would I have? If you'd once turned me down, I'm afraid I'd have just given up, and then where would we be?"

"I'm glad I didn't, then."

"So am I."

The squirrel had apparently given up on the pole and was employing a new tactic. Instead of trying to climb to the platform, he was hiding under a bush until a bird landed on the feeder, then rushing out, startling the bird into flying away and with any luck knocking some of the corn and seeds off the platform in the process.

"Do you think we should go back in?" Susan asked.

"That's where the liquor is."

"Good point. Let's go in, then."

He put his arm around her. "Have I mentioned lately that I love you?"

"No, but it's nice to be reminded."

IX

VERY LITTLE HAD CHANGED IN THE LIVING ROOM. George and Eric were still on the love seat, with Ellen sitting on the arm closest to the bar, next to her brother. Jim was pacing in the middle of the room, looking annoyed. Karen hadn't moved since first sitting down on the couch when they arrived. There was no sign of Mark, so Bob presumed he'd be in the kitchen with his smartphone, checking up on his practice.

Bob thought he should keep his priorities straight, so he headed for the bar.

"I don't suppose," he said, "there's any hope you've all managed to resolve your differences while we were outside?"

George just shook his head and emptied his own glass. "Sorry," he said. "I'm still gay, and Jim is still sounding like Abin Cooper on a bad day."

Bob put four ice cubes in his glass and poured in the blended Scotch. "Jim, he's your brother. You're supposed to love him."

"I do love him. But he's a sinner, and a sodomite, and we're commanded to hate the sin, no matter how we may feel about the sinner." He sat down on the couch next to his wife. "God allowed Bin Laden to kill thousands of people on 9/11 because this country was letting queers do whatever they liked to each other. There's absolutely no way anyone can deny that."

"Oh, of course they can deny it. Anyone who even thought about it would."

Susan was also busy at the bar. "Who's Abin Cooper?" she asked her husband.

"I have no idea."

Ellen laughed. "He's this insane fundamentalist preacher in *Red State*. It's a Kevin Smith movie. He kidnaps people he thinks are sinners, gays, kids looking to get laid, like that, and murders them in his church."

Susan looked a bit skeptical. "Good movie?"

"Satanic porno," Jim grunted.

Ellen ignored him. Jim thought *Victor/Victoria* was gay porn, and possibly a sign of the apocalypse. "It's pretty bloody, Mom. I don't think you'd like it, but, yes, pretty good."

"Here's how I see the situation," Bob said. "George and Eric are in love, and they would like to be married. My feeling about that is, fine, let them be married." He walked over to the love seat. "If the two of you have to move to New York to do so, also fine. We'll miss you, but Ohio doesn't have marriage equality yet and New York does. You're my son, I love you, and that's the important thing, not some ancient religious law meant for an entirely different time and place."

Jim was on his feet again. "Dad, you can't allow this!"

"Yes, Jim, I can." He sipped from his drink. "I really don't have a say in it—and neither do you. If your brother wants to marry Eric, and doesn't mind moving to a state where it's legal, then he can do just that."

"Dad, you're condemning my little brother to an eternity in hell."

"It seems to me you're the one who wants to do that."

"It's not what I want," Jim insisted. "It's what God wants."

Bob shook his head. "No, God just said, 'kill gay men if they have sex.' Or, at least, someone claimed that he did, which is probably even worse."

"'Their blood shall be upon them.' You know what that

means, don't you? It means that anything that happens to these perverts is their own fault. If they defy God, they can expect to be punished."

"By whom?"

"By God, obviously."

"Has he ever done that?"

"Done what?"

"Punished anyone. Has God ever actually punished anyone? Himself, I mean. I'm not talking about a group of people deciding that God wants someone punished and doing it for him. God doesn't really punish, you know. He just lets others do his dirty work for him. Or, really, they just do whatever *they* want to do and then claim it was God's will."

"You're getting pretty close to blasphemy, Dad."

"Blasphemy is a victimless crime."

"God won't be mocked, and he won't be defied without consequences. If not here, then in the afterlife. Hell is forever, Dad."

George looked up from the love seat. "So is stupidity, apparently."

The doorbell seemed unusually loud. Susan hurried to the front door, never more grateful to hear the familiar Westminster chimes.

"I don't know who this is," she said, "but every one of you, just shut up and be polite."

She swung the door open. Even if it was just a parcel being delivered, it was something to interrupt the rancor. What it was, rather surprisingly, was Bob's secretary.

"Hi."

"Hi, Carol," Susan responded. "Come on in."

Carol stepped into the room, stopping suddenly when she noticed all the people. They didn't look too happy, she thought.

"It looks like you have company," Carol said, starting to back up. "I could come back later."

"Just family," Susan told her. "Do you know our kids?"

"I think maybe I've seen him somewhere," she answered, looking at Jim. "But I don't think I've ever met any of them."

Susan took Carol's arm and began to move her around the room as she made the introductions. "The familiar looking one is our eldest son, Jim. You've probably seen him on TV. And this is Karen, his wife. Then Ellen, over there, our daughter, and the good looking young fellow who just wandered in from the kitchen is her husband, Mark. This is our other son, George, and his roommate, Eric. You know Bob, obviously. Family, this is Carol Burgess, Bob's secretary at the college."

"Nice to meet you guys," Carol muttered.

"Eric isn't really my roommate," George offered. "He's my fiance."

"Oh?" This was interesting.

"You know damned well that isn't true, George," Jim shouted. "Queers can't get married."

I need more booze, Bob thought. "So much," he sighed, "for any hope of a peaceful interlude."

"I could go," Carol offered.

Bob shook his head. "No, stay. Those two have been at it ever since George and Eric arrived. I expect they'll continue until one or the other leaves, or until Jim has an epiphany and decides to stop taking his moral cues from a homophobic, bronze age shepherd."

"I was hoping that company might shut them up," Susan said. "I guess I was wrong."

Ellen was back at the bar, making fresh drinks for Mark and herself. "Yes, why can't you all be quiet. George is who he is, and Jim is who he is, and if you can't get along, just shut up, or talk about something you actually do agree on."

"Not much of that," George said. "Baseball, maybe."

James looked at him disgustedly. "You're moving to New York. Probably turn into a damned Yankees fan."

"Not likely. I'm with Dad on that one. It will always be the Indians."

55

Eric chuckled softly. "Well, the Mets, maybe."

"Oh, shut up, faggot," Jim shouted, turning toward him. "This is probably all your fault anyway."

"What do you mean, my fault?"

"I know how you guys work. The way you like to lure the innocent into your web of sin and perversion."

"Sin and perversion!" Eric repeated, sounding somehow like the perfect Southern Baptist preacher on a real stem winder. He turned to George. "Does he think he's on television here?"

"Probably." George walked up to Jim, who backed away slightly. George was the younger brother, but he was by far the stronger of the two. Looking at them, there was no trouble telling who had been the quarterback and who had been the worst player on the golf team.

"I knew I was gay in grade school, Jim. Eric had nothing to do with it. I only met him a few months ago, and if anybody seduced anybody, I seduced him."

Ellen banged on the ice bucket with the tongs. "Will you two just knock it off?"

"Yes," Karen said, much more loudly than usual, "please."

Jim looked over at her with a look that would cow most people. "Karen, you stay out of this." It sounded like, "I'll deal with you later."

"Let her talk if she wants to," his father growled.

It was well past time to change the subject, Susan decided. "So, Carol, what brings you here today."

"Oh, nothing all that important, really. I can see you have your hands full this afternoon. I think my news can wait."

"News?" Susan perked up. "No, news is probably a good thing. Do you think it will provide a distraction from this religious war we're having?"

"Maybe." But it will probably cause other problems. "But it can wait."

Bob sat in his chair. "What's going on, Carol?"

"Yes, tell us," Susan urged. Anything to end the fighting.

"Well... I'm pregnant."

Bob felt a sudden, urgent need to finish his drink, which was still nearly full. He swallowed it all anyway, almost choking.

"Oh," Susan said, "interesting."

Bob looked over at the two woman, who were now seated next to Karen on the couch. "Really?" He decided not try to say any more. He usually didn't sound like a soprano.

"Did you know about this?" Susan asked.

"What could I possibly know? Uh, no."

Jim was suddenly all smiles. "I'll bet your husband's happy," he said, reverting to the 'friendly' pastor.

"I don't have a husband."

Reverend Friendly was gone as quickly as he had arrived. "This house just seems to be very attractive to sinners today. You need to get one, young lady. You tell that father he needs to marry you right now!"

"I don't think I can."

Susan was looking pointedly at her husband. "I don't either. I'm sort of thinking he might already be taken."

Bob looked at his suddenly empty glass and stood up, heading for the bar and taking the long way around the room. As far from his loving bride as he could manage. "Shouldn't we be getting lunch on the table?" he asked. "Anyone need a drink?"

Susan smiled. "You can make one for me while you're at it. Dad."

Carol looked down at her feet. "I said it could wait."

Ellen looked at both her parents. Their expressions were interesting, and she was sure she'd seen the same ones on her students at times. So that meant... "Oh, shit!"

Mark nudged her. "Maybe we should leave, huh?"

Susan got up and faced everyone. "No one is leaving. We're going to celebrate this anniversary like Farragut at Mobile Bay. Damn the torpedoes, full speed ahead!"

X

THERE HADN'T BEEN ANY CELEBRATING. Not just then, and not during the next ten minutes. The three kids, if they could still be called that, had realized things were really tense when their father took off his jacket, opened his waistcoat, undid his tie, and unbuttoned his collar. He really wasn't a casual sort of person. Not before supper, at least.

Now he was out on the porch with Carol, leaving Susan to deal with things in the living room. He couldn't help wondering how that was going. They'd both had numerous affairs over the years, but so far as he knew none of their children were aware of it.

Well, he thought, so much for that last remaining bit of innocence.

"You're absolutely sure of this?" he asked. It was hard not to hope that the pregnancy was just a late period. It happened. It had happened more than once with Susan.

"I did the test three times. I'm definitely pregnant."

"Wonderful."

Carol leaned against the porch railing and looked out over the yard, her eyes momentarily resting on the cross street neighbor's election sign. No way was she going to vote for that guy.

"Your wife doesn't seem too happy."

"We can hardly expect her to be, can we?

"I suppose not." She frowned. "It sure didn't take her long to figure it out."

"Yes. Well, I don't suppose I've been the most faithful husband who ever lived. I've strayed over the years..." *How many times?* he wondered. *Too many to keep straight, it seemed.* "But I always come back. I'm not going to leave her, you know."

Carol shrugged. "I'm not going to ask you to."

"Certainly makes the decision on retirement, though," he said, mostly to himself. "I'll have to keep working to make the support payments."

"I'm not asking for that, either."

Or so you think. "Perhaps not, but you will eventually. Or if you don't, the state will do it for you. You *are* planning to keep it, aren't you?"

"I think so. Should I?"

"Not for me to say."

"Why not? It'll be your kid."

Bob started pacing, walking behind her along the length of the porch. "It's *your* body. Children are wonderful. I love mine very much. But you've seen enough of what's going on inside right now to recognize that at times they can also be a gigantic pain in the arse."

"One of them seems to think I'm going to hell for this."

"Oh, Jim thinks damn near everyone is going to hell for *something*. Ignore him; he's an idiot."

"I've seen him on TV. There seem to be a lot of things he doesn't like. My mom likes him, though. She keeps sending him money to pray for me."

"Yes, he's rather fond of money, I think. But he hates sin, too, so naturally he hates anything that might be at all enjoyable."

"I think we *do* qualify as sinners. There's that whole adultery thing to consider."

"We can always look at the way Jesus would have."

"I don't think he would have approved, either," Carol said. After working for him for several years, she was familiar with Bob's background. Her own family was from Tennessee, and affiliated with a Holiness Church. Sunday school, Wednesday evening prayer meetings and Bible study, and a firm conviction that sin was inborn and only to be conquered by constant prayer, study, and giving money to the church and every itinerant evangelist who came to town. She'd been more than glad to get out of there when the chance came, but she'd had a pretty thorough religious education.

What passed for one in her home town, at least.

"He was Jewish, so he would have used a Jewish definition of the crime. Turns out, in Jewish law, only the woman's marital status matters. You're single." He smiled. "In Biblical days, Jewish men were allowed to have more than one wife at a time, but women could only have one husband. You could only commit adultery with a *married* woman."

"So no one is going to take us out and throw rocks at us?"

"I shouldn't worry about that."

You don't know *my* family, Carol thought. "They don't really do that any more, do they?"

Bob really couldn't help being a teacher. He'd been doing it for nearly four decades. "According to the Talmud, they never did. My Jewish friends—very highly educated ones at that—have related that one of Judaism's proudest achievements is that, despite having a horribly strict punishment for adultery, no one has ever been executed for it. Apparently the rules of evidence you'd have to follow in order to get a conviction make it impossible."

Others, he thought, weren't so scrupulous. Arabs still stoned people to death, though according to his scholarly Jewish friends, they didn't do it correctly. The process was intended to be painless, not a form of torture. The *first* rock was supposed to kill the victim, and its shape and weight were carefully specified, as was point of impact and distance thrown.

The chief accuser was also required to throw it, which tended to discourage the accusations.

"So, you think I should keep the baby?"

"Your decision." My participation in this event, he thought, might have amounted to a few minutes and one out of thirty or forty million sperm produced that day. How much say should I really have in it?

"Your wife does seem to be taking it all pretty calmly, all things considered."

"Wait until she's had a few more drinks." He smiled, thinking he'd like a few more himself. "And the battle between Jim and George has her a little preoccupied, too."

"What do you think she'd say? Keep the baby, or get rid of it?"

"I'd expect about the same as me. Do whatever you can to avoid becoming pregnant in the first place, but once you are, go ahead and have the baby." He shrugged. "Unless there's a good reason not to."

"No pro-life rants?"

"That's Jim's department."

Along with my mother's, Carol thought. It had been hard enough telling Bob. How the hell was she going to tell her mother? By phone, most likely. It was probably safer.

"I'm keeping the baby," she said. "This isn't exactly the way I wanted to start a family, but I do want to have children. I just wish the circumstances were different."

Understandable, Bob thought. "You mean, where the father was someone who could actually *be* the father? Someone you could marry, and who could help you raise the kid?"

"That would be nice."

"I really *am* the father?"

"No one else it could be."

"You mean to say there are no eligible young men panting after you that you could talk into marriage?"

"Not a single one. No one has even asked me out in the last six months. Why do you think I went after you in the first place?"

"They tell me I have a sexy accent."

"The French have sexier ones. You were just horny and available."

"I still find it a little hard to believe that you just couldn't get a date. You're a beautiful young woman. I'd think men would be lined up around the block wanting to buy you diamond rings. Or, at least, supper."

"One guy claimed I intimidated him. Said he figured anyone who looked like me had to be taken. You men are all so damned insecure."

"We are that. It's something I told Susan earlier today. I was so scared she'd turn me down that I very nearly didn't ask her out on that first date. Stupid, looking back."

"You're a man. Stupid is just normal."

XI

JIM LOOKED DOWN AT HIS MOTHER, who was seated in her regular place in one of the two easy chairs facing the television. She had another drink in her hand.

"What do you suppose they're talking about out there?" he asked.

"Nothing that concerns you."

"He's my father. Of course it concerns me."

"He's my husband. It concerns me more."

"So what do you plan to do about it?"

Susan frowned. "The same thing I always do. Have another drink."

"That's not going to help anything."

"If you have enough to drink, it all seems to matter less."

Jim walked over to the window, but couldn't see his father through it. They must be over at the far end of the porch, he thought.

"The college should fire the little slut," he declared.

Karen looked over at her husband. He never changes, she thought. You either meet his standards or he just writes you off. "Why do you think she's a slut, Jim?" she demanded. "Do you think single women *want* to get pregnant? How do you know your father isn't to blame?"

"Nobody asked your opinion, Karen."

"Yet it's a perfectly good opinion," George interjected.

"That's a big part of your problem, Jim. You just presume that everyone is essentially evil. You figure they're all hopeless sinners, so they'll naturally be to blame if something goes wrong."

He took a long swallow of his drink before continuing. "But the world doesn't always conform to your fantasies. Just like you presume that any unmarried woman who gets pregnant has to be a slut—as if it just isn't possible for her to be entirely innocent. Just because you have sex without being married doesn't make you an immoral person."

"It does in this world," Jim insisted.

Karen stood up suddenly, glaring at her husband. "No, Jim, it doesn't."

"I told you to shut up."

"Not this time." This was a new experience for everyone, not the least for Karen. She hadn't overtly disagreed with her husband since very early in their marriage. Before he'd made the consequences so obvious.

"What?"

"I said, 'not this time.' I'm your wife, not your slave."

"Good for you, Karen," George said, grinning.

"You can shut up, too, faggot."

"Jim!" All three of her children looked at Susan, startled. They hadn't heard that exact tone of voice since they were little, and back then it had never led to anything good. It was one step down from 'James Phillip Anderson,' and a reminder that corporal punishment was still acceptable in some households.

Karen turned to Susan. "Mom, do you think I could stay here with you and Dad for a few days?"

"I suppose so, but why?"

"Will Dad still be here?" Ellen asked. It seemed like a reasonable question.

"Damn right he will." Susan frowned, then smiled. It was the sort of smile that, when you saw it, tended to make you nervous. "He's not getting out of this that easily. But, Karen, why do you want to stay here? It's liable to be a little noisy around here for a while."

Karen nodded. She wasn't quite sure. Jim's family was, really, the only family she had. But would they want her hanging around after what she had finally decided to do?

"I think I need to become an Ohio resident," she said. "I also need to find a good lawyer, and that's probably going to take some time. I don't think I can do it in Texas." She looked at Jim. "He'd find a way to stop me."

Karen walked over to her husband, standing in front of him. "I think you can expect to be served with divorce papers sometime in the next few weeks. Let's see what those holy rollers of yours think of that. See what your TV audience thinks of it, for that matter. Won't they just love seeing your name all over the tabloids when they buy their groceries? 'Evangelist Jim Anderson Hauled into Divorce Court.' Oh, they'll just *love* that."

Jim was just about as mad as he'd ever been, but he decided to suppress it for the moment and just present her with simple reality.

"You can't divorce me," he said. "I won't allow it."

"It's not up to you," Karen said.

"Of course it is."

"Your wife is right," Eric interjected. "You can contest a divorce, but you'd just be wasting your time and money. If one party wants out of a marriage, and the other doesn't, the one who wants out will eventually prevail. That's just how it works."

James looked at his brother's partner in disgust. "And just what would you know about it, you goddamned homo?"

Eric shook his head. "It's what I do for a living, remember? One of my specialties is taking self-righteous pricks like you for every penny they have." He looked at Jim's suit. Custom tailoring, an expensive wool fabric. "And you seem to have a lot of pennies."

"Well," Jim declared, "she can't have a divorce. I haven't

committed adultery, and I'm pretty sure she hasn't, either. Have you?"

Karen glared at him. "Of course not."

Jim's smile was triumphant. "See? No adultery, no divorce. Jesus said so."

Eric couldn't help laughing. "What makes you think a judge is going to care what Jesus said? He's only going to care about what's in the statute books." He turned to Karen. "If you need a lawyer, we can talk. I think I might just enjoy cleaning out this asshole."

"Oh, yeah," James growled, "you like assholes, don't you, queer?"

Karen looked at her husband. The public Jim was utterly absent now. This was the private Jim. The bitter, hateful zealot who would entertain no notion that conflicted with his own.

"Eric, you're on," she said. She shook her head. "But you won't get much out of him. There's almost nothing in his name. There's a corporation that owns the church and our house, and another owns the TV studio and his show. He gets a salary of about $20,000 a year, and the corporations pay his expenses. I suppose they also deduct them."

Eric nodded. He'd handled a minister's divorce once before and found the same sort of setup. "They're probably set up as non-profits, so they don't have to pay taxes."

The church certainly would be. Churches were easy. They didn't even have to justify their status, or file all the reports the IRS required of any other non-profit corporation. All they had to do was say, "we're a church," and non-profit status was instantly granted.

"Don't worry, though," Eric said. "You'll still get what's coming to you. We can find the money. We'll just have to convince the court that the corporations aren't what they're held out to be. That they're just set up to hide his personal assets, and avoid taxes. We may even be able to get him on tax fraud. He wouldn't be the first evangelist to end up in jail for not paying his taxes."

"Fat chance," Jim laughed. "We live in Texas. And I know every judge in the Dallas area.

Eric shrugged. "We'll be filing in Ohio, Jimmy. Karen just needs to live here for six month to establish residence. After that, Ohio courts have jurisdiction. Hell, you might even be better off this way. Texas is a community property state—Ohio isn't. If she divorced you in Texas, she'd get half of everything."

"Do you really need to do this?" Susan asked. "You've been together eight years. I thought you were happy." She had a sudden thought. "And I don't want my son going to prison, either."

"Jim was happy," Karen said. "At least, I think he was. My job was just to do as I was told, and be the dutiful little preacher's wife. I was supposed to sit in the front pew in church and smile, or stand beside him during the family segments of his show. I had to read my lines off the cue card with just the right combination of sincerity and empathy. I learned to fake both. As long as I did all that to his satisfaction, and anything else he wanted, he wouldn't need to punish me."

"What do you mean, punish?" Ellen asked. Automatic suspicion on hearing that sort of statement was a part of teacher training.

"Are you saying he hit you?" Susan asked. "Something like that?"

Karen nodded. "That's exactly what he'd do, Mom."

"If you're divorcing me," Jim huffed, "you can't call her 'mom' anymore."

"Shut up, Jim."

"If he's been hitting you…" Ellen said, suspiciously.

Karen nodded slowly. "But only when I deserved it," she said. "You know, if I disagreed with him, or something like that. But he was careful. He never hit me anywhere it would show. I guess that's a lot easier when you make sure your wife dresses in a good, modest Christian way."

She took off her jacket, glaring at her husband as she did so, and pulled up the right sleeve of her white silk blouse.

There was a large, livid purple bruise on her upper arm, along with the fading remains of earlier bruising. "Modest clothing," she said, "covers more than just naked flesh."

James moved with surprising speed, swinging a clenched fist at his wife. Karen instinctively flinched, but this time George and Eric were there to get in the way.

James looked at the two of them and decided that was a fight he wasn't going to win. With an inarticulate snarl, he stomped off through the door leading to the hallway. A moment later a door slammed.

"Hiding in the bathroom," Ellen said. It was what he'd always done when they were children, any time he got upset about something.

"You know," Mark whispered to Ellen, "I'm not very comfortable with this."

"I don't think anyone is."

"No, I mean I'm really not comfortable with this. I don't like conflicts."

"No one does, Mark."

"I think we should leave."

Ellen shook her head. Confront her husband with a life threatening medical emergency and he'd become icy calm, taking charge and getting everyone through the mess. Anything else, even something as minor as a surly convenience store clerk, and he was hopeless.

"We can't leave yet," she said. "George and Eric, and especially Karen, are going to need all the support they can get. Mom, too, I think."

"You're sure?"

"I'm sure." She looked at him sternly, as if she were confronting one of her pupils. She knew he'd give in. He couldn't take the idea of any conflict with her, either.

"Well, okay, but..."

Susan stared down the hallway. What was going on here? she wondered. She also wondered at her own feelings. This was a dispute between her son and her daughter-in-law, and obviously she *should* be reacting like a mother and defending her own offspring.

Except her offspring had just took a swing at his wife, and how could she defend that? Where had that even come from? He certainly hadn't learned it from his father. Bob obviously had his faults, but a tendency toward violence wasn't one of them. The philosopher, she supposed. He had a tendency to overanalyze things, so that by the time it occurred to him that violence *might* be in order, the opportunity had long passed. He'd never hit the kids, and he'd certainly never hit her.

No, her sympathies had to be with Karen on this. Hitting women was too far beyond the pale.

"I think Jim is just insecure," Susan told her daughter-in-law. "Really insecure." She frowned. Was this a defense? She shook her head. "That's no excuse, but it might be an explanation. He wasn't like this growing up."

George snorted. "Yeah, he was. Just never where you'd find out about it."

"No one ever said anything," Susan protested. "Not you, not his teachers, not his friends' parents."

George tried to think of a way of explaining it she'd understand. He decided TV might help here. "How much do you think Mrs. Haskell knew about Eddie's behavior? He was a little angel whenever he thought there was a chance of being caught."

When all else fails, George thought, you could still leave it to Beaver to get your point across.

Karen only vaguely remembered the show from reruns, but she got the point. "Jim's afraid of a lot of things," she said, "and people finding out what he's really like is one of them. I know that. But I just can't keep doing this. I'm tired of being told that my opinions don't matter. I'm tired of being told that he's the boss in the family, and that I'm just supposed to do whatever he says and never question it, because Saint Paul said that's how it has to be. I'm tired of being hit. I'm just tired of *him*, when you come right down to it."

"Lots of scared people today," Susan muttered.

"What?"

"Nothing. Just something Bob said earlier."

"About Jim?" Karen queried.

"About himself. You wouldn't know it, to watch him in front of a class, or on a lecture platform, but he's really very shy."

Ellen found herself looking at the front door. Her father and his secretary, or, she supposed, girl friend, was on the other side. Talking? Doing whatever they did when they were alone on a porch. "Apparently not shy enough," she remarked.

"Jim isn't shy at all," Karen said. "He's scared, but not shy. I don't think he could ever be anything but totally religious—thinking for himself would require too much effort. It's so much easier if the answers are all provided."

Susan nodded. "Bob probably thinks too much. I'd say it might be better if he let himself be a little more impulsive." She smiled wanly, looking at the front door. "But that doesn't always work out, either."

Eric injected himself into the awkward silence. "Hey," he said, "I should probably apologize to you guys. I think I sort of went into court mode there for a minute. I'm really socialized better than that. It's just that guys like that really get to me. I don't like bullies." He smiled at George. "From what he's told me, George didn't have it too bad in high school. Big shot athlete and all. And the straight kids didn't know he was gay, so they didn't pick on him. The bullies knew I was gay, and I wasn't this big back then. If you think lockers are ugly from the outside, you should see them from the inside."

George draped an arm around Eric's shoulders. "Right. Jim would have been after me if he'd known. Hell, he picked on straight kids because he *thought* they were gay. Just because a guy was bad at sports and liked being in plays didn't make him gay, but Jim couldn't get that through his thick skull. Him and his, 'We get to beat you up because Jesus said we should' buddies."

Karen looked at the two men. "I think you're probably one of the things Jim is afraid of," she said. "So is losing his job, or, not so much his job, but his power over his congregation and all those people who watch him on television every day and send in all that money."

George nodded, smiling. "You're a nice kid. Honestly, I never understood why you married him in the first place. And he's, what, eleven years older than you?"

Karen sighed. "He can be nice when he wants to. And at the time it seemed like a pretty good idea. My life was kind of messed up back then. It's still pretty messed up, but not the same way."

"What do you mean?" Susan asked.

"You know my parents died when I was twelve, right?"

Susan nodded. "A car accident, wasn't it?"

"Right. Some stupid high school kid who shouldn't have been drinking in the first place. That's why I don't drink."

Ellen looked at her curiously. "I thought that was a religious thing."

"No," Karen said, shaking her head, "it's a personal thing. That kid didn't just kill my mom and dad, he pretty well killed what should have been my life, too."

She didn't really remember the crash. Her parents had been in the front seats and died. She'd been belted into the left rear seat and survived. But she didn't know that until a day later, when she woke up in the hospital.

Except for a concussion that had left her unconscious for fourteen hours, she hadn't been physically injured. The worst shock was realizing that, with her parents dead, she no longer had a home to return to.

"You see," she continued, "there's a big problem with being orphaned at twelve. You're too old. No one wants to adopt a girl that age —they want babies. They want someone who's never had parents, not someone who remembers them all too well. So I wound up in the foster system."

"Not one of the better placements, I take it?" Eric asked.

"The first two families were okay. I think I was pretty numb, but you get over people dying. I guess we're just made that way. We have to be, don't we? I wasn't their kid, but they treated me okay. But the family they placed me with when I turned 16 was something else. The only reason they wanted me there was because they got paid. Me and four other kids. And when I turned 18, they didn't exactly celebrate. All it meant to them was that the checks would stop coming once I finished high school. Once I was 18, I think their only goal was to get me the hell out of their house as soon as I got that diploma in my hand."

George touched her shoulder. He took his hand away at once, noticing the involuntary flinch at his touch. Jim really *has* done a job on this poor kid, he thought.

"How did Jim get involved in this?" he asked.

"He was already pastor at his church by then. My foster family were members." She frowned. "Still are, for that matter. Anyway, Jim was 29, and some of the members were wondering why he wasn't married yet. So my 'family' started pushing me at him. I'd just turned 18, and I was still a virgin, which was apparently important to Jim."

And not even for the usual religious reasons, she'd later discovered. Jim had somewhere got the idea that it was necessary to marry a virgin for safety reasons. Everyone who ever had unmarried sex, he sincerely believed, always caught some sort of venereal disease the first time they did. If you had sex with anyone who wasn't a virgin, you'd catch something that would kill you. School sex-ed classes didn't teach this obvious truth, which was one reason he opposed sex education in schools. That, and teaching kids about sex obviously caused them to immediately go out and start fucking each other.

"Also, back then, I guess I was just used to doing what I was told, so when Jim proposed I went along. It would get me out of that house. It just didn't occur to me that it wouldn't be much of an improvement. I was moving from a grubby room in a split level into a mansion. I'd get away from that family, too."

"Did you love him?" Ellen asked.

"Something like that. I was 18, what did I know about love?"

Down the hall a door opened. Jim came back, looking much calmer, but no less angry. He walked over to Karen, standing in front of her, just that little bit too close, trying to intimidate her by his sheer physical presence.

It didn't work as well as he'd hoped. He was six feet tall, and weighed no more than 180 pounds. His wedge shaped torso and broad shoulders were mostly careful tailoring. And as his wife was only three inches shorter, and wearing heels, looking "down" at her meant looking down no more than half an inch at most.

"So," he said, "have you got this foolishness out of your head yet?"

Karen shook her head, then looked him directly in the eye. "You can go back to Texas whenever you want, Jim. I'm staying here."

"You'll come back to Texas where you belong."

"I told you, I'm done letting you push me around."

"She has the right to do whatever she wants, Jim," Ellen asserted. "And you're in no position to try to stop her. It's not like it used to be. Cops arrest guys like you now. They don't just tell them to go take a walk around the block and cool off."

Karen laughed. "They do in Texas. At least, they do if the guy happens to be their pastor. In our town, that's how it is, more often than not. The last time, though, he almost ended up getting hauled in until that sergeant showed up and told the patrolman to let it go."

Jim shook his head. "Eddie knows me," he sneered. "He wasn't going to let that damned wetback pull that shit on me. Not on a real American."

Karen looked at the others and shrugged. Her husband really was an idiot.

"He's not a wetback, Jim," she said, turning back to him. "Officer Mendoza's family was living in Texas before Sam Houston's grandfather was born." She looked at the others again, explaining. "But, you see, he's a Catholic, so a big-time

Protestant preacher doesn't intimidate him. I guess Catholic cops don't feel the same sort of holy awe and divine willingness to overlook stuff that Jim gets from his own members."

XII

BOB WAS LEANING with his hands on the porch railing, looking out across the front yard. The street was quiet. At this time of day cars were rare.

"I'm not really sure what to do next," Carol said quietly.

"Nor am I," Bob admitted. "The situation is unprecedented."

She looked at him curiously. "My impression was that your wife didn't think this was unusual."

Bob straightened up. He smiled weakly, shrugging. "It's the pregnancy that's unprecedented," he said. "Previously, the consequences have been limited to a good deal of shouting, recriminations, and the consumption of considerable quantities of alcohol. And, of course, I found myself sleeping alone for a while."

"No one ever got pregnant before?"

"No, not before."

"And our little affair is over?"

"I think that might be a safe presumption. At least, the sexual part of it. Financially, I don't suppose it will be ending any time soon."

Carol frowned. "I don't want your money. When did I ever ask for money?"

"Your desires may not matter. Unless you get yourself married post haste, there will likely come a time when you need some sort of assistance. Once that happens, the state will insist on knowing who fathered your child. You'll have to tell them."

"What if I don't want assistance?"

"I know how much the college pays you. It's not going to support two people very well. And if you ask for help, the state will decide on a support amount, and then come after me to pay it. Retroactively, I might add." He shrugged. "The problem with knowing a lot of lawyers is you learn this stuff."

Carol began pacing the length of the porch. Her arms were folded in front of her.

"No one wants to marry me," she said. "You can't. Even if you wanted to. Which you don't."

He spread his arms and sat on the railing. "I do care for you, but I already have a wife. Human nature, you see, is much too predictable. There are those we love briefly, and those we love forever. Sometimes there are both at once."

"I presume I'm briefly?"

Walked right into that one, he thought. "I'm too old for you anyway. I'm 64, you're 25. That works for a fling, or possibly in fiction, but it doesn't bode well for a long-term relationship. If it did, believe me, you'd see a lot more old men with very young wives."

Carol stopped pacing and looked at him. "You see some."

"And the old men are generally rather well off. A full professor makes an adequate living, but not the sort of living that comes with young trophy wives."

"All women aren't after money, you know." She was sure she wasn't. She wasn't after a baby, either, but it certainly looked like she was getting one of those.

"I don't think you're falling in love with me, either," Bob said. "No, I think the basis of our relationship, beyond the professional one, was more one of convenience than passion."

"So, I was horny and you were handy? Is that it?"

"I'd say that worked in both directions."

"Sometimes," Carol said, "you can be a little too cold and logical."

"I'm a very passionate person," Bob said, in a matter of fact tone. "This is simply what passion looks like in an Englishman of my age. It's the public school education. It does not train one to be demonstrative."

What is it I like about this man? Carol asked herself. He's actually fairly average looking. Well preserved might be the right term. He was 64, but looked more like a man in his mid-50s. And he was very good in bed. Not a spectacular lover. Not someone who generated overwhelming passions and set off huge fireworks displays.

He cared as much about what she experienced as what happened to him. That was it, she thought. Too many young guys were only concerned with themselves.

"I don't really want to take you away from your wife," she said. A small part of her did, but mostly she recognized that he was right on that score.

Bob shrugged. "She wouldn't let me go. And I do love her."

She shook her head slowly. "You're having an affair with me, but you love your wife?"

"I'm sorry, but yes. She even understands me."

"You're not too old for me, you know."

"Neither," Bob said, "am I really available. You're certain you have no one who'd be interested? Even if no one has asked you out recently, there must have been some who would have wanted a permanent relationship."

Well, she thought. "There was someone, but…"

"But?"

"Also not available."

The front door opened and Susan came partway out onto the porch. She looked a bit frazzled, Bob thought. Was something else going on? Or was it just having the kids there right now. The discovery of previous affairs had generally involved just the two of them.

"You two," Susan said. "Inside. Now."

"Oh, hell," Bob muttered.

"I should probably go," Carol offered.

"No," Susan snapped. "You just come inside, young lady."

This is how it feels when the bailiff comes out and tells you the jury has come back in with a verdict, Bob thought. I wonder if one of my children will be wearing the black cap.

XIII

THE TENSION WAS OBVIOUS as they came back inside. George and Eric were sitting together on the love seat. Both looked as if they were prepared to spring up at any instant, as if they were afraid of some problem and ready to address it through physical action.

Ellen was sitting on the arm of the couch, next to Karen, who had taken off her jacket. Ellen looked concerned. Karen, astonishingly, looked both angry and determined.

Mark was standing beside the bar, holding a very large drink.

Jim was pacing, but stopped as his father came in. He walked to the far side of the living room and stood there, his arms crossed. Bob couldn't tell if he was projecting anger, staunch determination, or the kind of tough facade some people adopted to hide their fears.

"Anything interesting happen while we were gone?" Bob asked.

Susan nodded. "Some. Jim is still trying to restart the Spanish Inquisition. George is doing a nice job of defending himself. We've discovered that Eric has a tendency to become extremely confrontational when he's working. Oh, and Karen is divorcing James.

All Bob could do for a moment was look at her. "You go outside for a few minutes…" he muttered.

"She says he beats her," Susan added.

"What? I thought we raised him better than that."

"So did I."

Bob walked over to the couch. "Karen, does Jim really hit you?"

She nodded, pulling up her sleeve again to display the bruising. "Yes," she said. "See?"

That Jim's expression was one of bluster masking fear was instantly obvious as his father stormed across the living room. He really was a coward at heart, Karen thought. She knew his father had never hit him, never would hit him, yet now he shrank back as if expecting a physical blow. It was only momentary, but she'd noticed it.

"Jim, what the hell is the matter with you?" Bob demanded. "We raised you to be a good man, and a good husband, not a wife beater."

"You should talk, with your pregnant bimbo standing there." Regain the moral high ground, Jim thought. Adultery was obviously worse than hitting your wife, or why was only one of them forbidden?

"Fine, I have cheated on my wife. But I've never hit her."

"The head of the woman is the man," Jim quoted.

Bob found himself looking up in exasperation. "That was 2,000 years ago," he said. "And I don't give a damn if you can find a hundred passages that say men are supposed to beat their wives to insure obedience. You're also supposed to have enough common sense to know that the entire notion is nothing but bullshit. If your moral guide tells you to do something your common sense says is immoral, then you bloody well don't do it."

"If it's in the Bible," Jim patiently explained, "it's moral."

It's like dealing with a two-year-old, Bob thought. "Even if you claim your source is divine, it was still written down by men, and men screw up — get things wrong. Faith is a belief in something you can't prove. You're supposed to be intelligent enough to know that sometimes the reason you can't prove it is because it's not real. Do you let yourself be guided by faith when you know it's wrong? Or when there's simply a more rational alternative?

"He certainly does," Karen said. "That's how he killed our son."

It was a good thirty seconds before anyone spoke. This was the first time anyone had ever suggested the baby had died of anything but a tragic illness.

"Morgan?" Susan said. "What do you mean, killed? I thought he died of an infection."

Karen nodded. "He did. A little scratch, and it got infected. So what does this man of God do? Does he call for a doctor? No, he prays over him. Jim and his holy friends in his holy inner circle pray for the infection to go away. An antibiotic would have taken care of it, the doctor said, if we'd taken him in sooner. But Jim wouldn't let me. Not until it was too late."

"Don't try to put that off onto me, woman," Jim shouted. "That was all you. If it wasn't for your lack of faith, he would have been healed. But you kept insisting we call a doctor, telling God you didn't really believe in him, in his power. That you'd rather put your trust in the methods of this world instead of trusting in the God who made you. Only God can heal; doctors just think they can.

Eric shook his head, looking at George, then at Karen. "The man's not just a religious nut," he said, "he's fucking insane. Karen, you'll definitely be better off without him."

Karen stood up. She wanted to run at Jim and beat the stupid out of him. She didn't, but she truly wanted to. Still, she could hurt him in other ways. Ways that might remind him that his power had never been quite as great as he thought.

"Why do you think I never got pregnant again?" she asked, looking directly at her husband. "I've been on the pill ever since Morgan died. There was no way I'd ever take the chance of bringing another child into this world for you to kill." She looked at the others. "Of course, I didn't dare tell Jim. Taking the pill is a sin, you know."

George was confused. Jim was a Protestant minister. Nondenominational, but still adamantly Protestant. Forbidding *all* birth control was a Catholic fetish.

"You should have turned him over to the cops," Eric said, "and let them deal with it. You're talking criminal negligence at the least. Maybe even manslaughter. Might even be second degree murder — deliberately taking an action that any reasonable person would recognize is likely to result in death."

"I couldn't," Karen said. "He told me I'd be the one they'd blame."

"And you believed him?"

She shrugged and walked back to the couch, slumping down at one end. "I did then. I guess I wasn't thinking right. All I could think about was that my son was dead, and people would blame me." She looked up, her eyes wet. "Enough of them did."

"It *was* your fault," Jim declared. "Now just stop this nonsense about a divorce. You know I love you, and you love me. God wants us together."

Bob smiled ruefully. "Have you ever noticed that whenever someone says God wants you to do something, it really means *he* wants you to do it?" He looked at Eric. "And I'm afraid you're wrong. There's almost certainly some idiotic law on the books that says a parent can let a child die of neglect, so long as that parent sincerely believes this is what God wants."

Eric nodded. "Like that new law in Tennessee that makes bullying in school illegal, unless the victim is gay? Then you get to bully him all you like as long as your religion says it's okay? Kids kill themselves because of that kind of shit."

"Exactly." Bob stuck his hands into his trouser pockets. He had no particular reason to do so. Just being English, he thought. He walked over to his daughter-in-law. "Karen, if you go back to Jim, you're crazy."

He turned suddenly, thrusting his face forward so quickly

that Jim jerked backwards. "As for you, Jim, where do you get the gall to try to put the blame on Karen? You know damned well it was your own stupid insistence on trying to pray away an infection that killed your son. Prayer hasn't been an effective way to treat infections since antibiotics were discovered. It wasn't effective before, for that matter, but nothing else worked either, so at least you were no worse off than if you did nothing. Now relying on prayer just means that you die."

"Do you think," Susan suggested, "that we could all just calm down here? This was supposed to be a quiet little family gathering to celebrate our anniversary."

"Yes," Ellen said, "why don't we try that?"

"That's what I came here for," George said. "A nice family get together."

"You came here to tell us you're a pervert," Jim snapped. "And now your girlfriend is trying to break up my marriage."

"You did that all by yourself," Karen growled. "He's just going to help with the paperwork."

Eric moved over to the couch and sat by Karen. "I'm starting to wonder if we need a protection order here. Does he own any guns?"

She looked at him strangely. "We live in Texas. What do you think?"

Eric nodded. "Then we should probably make sure someone takes them away from him until this is all over."

George stood up and walked over to his father. This was supposed to be a happy day, he thought. It didn't seem to be turning out that way. "Really, Dad," he said, "this isn't what I wanted. Maybe Eric and I should have waited until it was just you and Mom, but Jim would have had to find out eventually."

"I think I should probably go," Carol said, quietly.

"You're not going anywhere," Susan snapped. "If you weren't pregnant, I'd tell you to make yourself a drink."

Carol looked at her resignedly. "If I wasn't pregnant," she muttered, "you wouldn't be telling me to stay."

"Right, what about this, Dad?" James demanded. "You

preach to me about how I should treat my wife, and here you are having an affair with your secretary."

"It's not the same thing." It wasn't, was it? After all, Susan knew that he fooled around. So did she. He seriously doubted that Karen had gone into her marriage giving a blanket consent to being beaten.

"Well," Ellen said, "maybe it is, kind of. But hitting is probably worse."

"Your father and I will work this out," Susan said. "Just as we've always done."

"Oh, great! He's a serial adulterer." James sounded furious. Strangely, Bob found himself wondering how much of it was real and how much was acting. "At least," James asserted, "I've never been with another woman."

"No," Karen said, "you just beat up the one you have."

Bob had moved to the bar and went to pour himself another Scotch. I'm drinking when I'm angry, he thought. Best stick with the blended stuff. Good enough for getting drunk.

"Why don't you try thinking for yourself, Jim?" he asked. "Just because someone wrote something down two or three thousand years ago doesn't mean it's still right. Or that it was ever right, for that matter."

"If it's in the Bible, it's right. Period."

"Jim, you're an idiot."

"I know what God wants," Jim declared, "and it doesn't include men marrying each other. Anyway, what about that slut of secretary of yours?"

Carol, who was sitting in Bob's chair, picked up the bone china bud vase from the table. "Watch it, buster. I'm not a relative. It wouldn't bother me a bit to smash this vase over your head."

Susan grabbed the vase away from her. "Not one of my vases, you won't."

"Sue," Bob said, "I like your priorities."

"Oh, shut up, Bob. You haven't even made it *into* the dog house yet; you're still buried under it."

Bob sat on the arm of the love seat. He'd have to think about that one. Was it because the family was there? He and Susan had a fairly clear routine for whenever an affair was discovered. For some reason she seemed more than usually annoyed this time.

"Jim," Karen said, "you're a pretty poor excuse for a man. Now you're attacking someone you don't even know. She made a mistake. Okay, people make mistakes. You make mistakes. I know your parents never taught you to act this way. You were nice enough when you were courting me. What the hell happened?"

"It's the righteous who'll be saved first when the tribulation comes. It won't be the fornicators or sodomites. They'll burn forever in a lake of fire." Jim was in full preacher mode now. This was familiar territory. This was why politicians listened to him, why his blog posts were so heavily referenced by conservative Facebook posters.

Bob just shook his head. It was an old, familiar refrain. "How the hell do you know that? How the hell do you even know there's going to be a tribulation? Or a judgment day?

"Read Revelation, Dad."

"I've read it. Honestly, I think Saint John was smoking something illegal when he wrote that thing. Pale horses, and dragons, and lakes of fire. Thomas Jefferson was right about Revelation — he called it the ravings of a maniac."

"The end times are nearly here," Jim insisted. "You can see the signs. You'll see he was right."

"The only signs of the end times I've seen," Bob grunted, "are on billboards. John thought Nero was the Antichrist, and Nero's been dead since the year 68. John was simply wrong. It's nineteen hundred years later now, so maybe it's about time to admit you were wrong, too."

"Dad, George is going to hell, his boyfriend is going to hell, your secretary is going to hell, and more than likely you're going to be right there with them."

"Oh, I think we'll all do just fine," Bob replied. "I expect *you'll* spend some time in hell, though. It's not a place you go to after you're dead, to my way of thinking. It's something you create for yourself, right here in this life." He looked over at Karen, then back at his son. "You say you love your wife, but do you? Your idea of love seems to be that she belongs to you, that you can simply impose your will on her. For you, hell is going to be losing that power. You're going to be really miserable when she's gone, and I just hope she has the good sense to stay gone."

Jim snorted. He started turning his wedding ring on his finger. Bob wondered if reality was starting to sink in.

"Don't worry," Jim said, "she'll be back. After a little while she'll miss the house and the cars and all the stuff that made her life so easy. She'll be back."

Bob looked pointedly at Karen. "I really hope she's smarter than that."

"She's a woman," Jim declared. "It's her role to serve. That's the problem, you know. God intends people to fill their natural roles, and people like you are encouraging them to go against nature, so you get women acting like men and men acting like women."

"That's not the problem," Bob said. "But I do know what *your* real problem is."

"What's that, Dad?"

"Your real problem is that you're a self-righteous, obnoxious, unimaginative, little fundamentalist prick."

Jim found himself balling his fists. Was he going to hit his father? No, there was certainly something in the Bible against doing that. Or was it that his father was an inch taller than he, and despite being 35 years older and drinking too much, very likely in better shape. There were those old pictures on the mantle, too. Pictures of a eighteen-year-old version of his father during his brief military service. He could remember being a young child and hearing why the parachutist's badge he was wearing was different from the ordinary sort. Definitely not someone to get into a fight with.

"I've had enough of this," he declared. "Karen, come on!"

She stood up, looked him up and down, and removed her wedding and engagement rings, dropping them into his hand. "Just go," she said.

He muttered something inarticulate and stomped out of the house, leaving the front door swinging open.

They could hear the car door slam, and his rented SUV starting up.

I guess I am staying here for a while, Karen thought.

XIV

KAREN WALKED OVER TO THE DOOR and closed it. "I feel like singing something," she said. "Something very happy. I won't tomorrow. I'm afraid he's right about one thing—I actually will miss him. He could be nice enough when he wanted to."

She walked back to the couch and sat down. "How do you remind yourself that the good times don't outweigh the bad?"

"It's called selective memory," Bob said. Sometimes reverting to the philosophy professor was the obvious course. "We seem to be programmed to remember the good things and forget the bad ones. That's how psychics work. They're just guessing, but somehow you only remember when they were right, and after a while you start to think they're *usually* right. You could easily have the same problem."

"I'll remember when Jim was nice, and forget about when he hit me? Like that?"

"Exactly."

She nodded, sinking back into the cushions. "Maybe if my parents had lived... I might have married someone else. Or gone to college."

"You can always do that," Susan said.

"Jim wouldn't like that."

"You're divorcing him," George said. "His opinion doesn't matter."

Karen sighed. "I know. But somehow it does, too. I've never been on my own, really. Well, maybe. That last foster family I might as well have been."

"You shouldn't let him get away with what he did to your son," Eric offered. "You were the one who wanted to take him to the doctor. Your husband is the irresponsible one, not you."

"I was nineteen when that happened," she said. "Jim was still the one who'd saved me from my foster family. Especially from my so-called 'dad.' Jim was still fairly gentle then. Still the benign authority figure. And he could point to all sorts of examples where prayer had healed someone. Just watch television, you'll see it. There's this big, super-famous evangelist, and he's praying and the next thing he tells you some woman in Illinois was just healed of breast cancer. You're supposed to believe. And send money. Send money and pray, and he can show you where someone was healed."

Bob snickered. It was a common enough story, and it was never true. "He can point to a coincidence, you mean?"

"Right," George said. "If a disease doesn't kill you, you generally get better even if you don't do anything."

"And about one out of every hundred cancer patients will go into spontaneous remission," Bob added. "So if Jim or some other preacher is going to claim this is because God decided to save that particular patient, it does rather beg the question of why he decided to kill the other 99. Of course, you're not supposed to talk about that. No, for my money, go with a doctor; the outcome is generally better."

"I think I said something like that to Jim," Karen admitted. "That's when he started hitting me. Before he'd just scold. Or remind me of how he'd given me all these things, and I should be grateful. Fine, I lived in a big house, and I had a nice car to ride around in. But his idea of love wasn't exactly the same as mine. I wanted someone who cared for me because I was me, not because he thought I looked good standing next to him in front of the congregation. Or because he thinks that being married is just the way a pastor is supposed to be.

Ellen had been listening. The more she heard, the less she liked her brother. "I'd have been out of there the first time he hit me," she said. "Or I'd have just killed him."

She looked rather pointedly at Mark when she said that. He just smiled.

"You had parents who cared about you," Karen replied. "I didn't after I was twelve. I was never close to any of the fosters, except that last foster father. And I'd have been a lot happier *not* to be close to him. Not *that* close, anyway."

"How close…"

"I don't want to talk about it." Karen looked across the room at the closed door. She wondered if Jim was going to get over his snit and come crawling back, or if he'd pointed the rented SUV north and was on his way back to Cleveland and the airport.

"What is love, anyway?" she asked.

"Caring," Ellen said. "Wanting to be with someone more than you want anything else."

"Knowing there's someone in the world who thinks you're the most important human being on the planet," Eric suggested.

"Love is just love," George said. "You know it when you find it."

"That's what I needed to learn," Karen sighed. "Before I could stand up to Jim, I had to somehow convince myself that what I wanted was just as important as what he wanted. That there was more to life than just doing as you're told. That I was allowed to have my own opinions. My own thoughts. Ultimately, that I could say I did *not* kill my son. That's what I realized, sitting there listening to my husband attacking Carol. It wasn't my fault, and I just couldn't let him get away with laying all that guilt on another person." She frowned, looked across the room at Carol. "For all I know, maybe it *is* her fault, but I really don't know, and Jim damn sure doesn't know."

"Thanks," Carol said. "I guess."

"He hates a lot of people," Karen continued. "He says it's God who hates them, but it's really just Jim. George, you and Eric scare the hell out of him. You're gay. You're comfortable with that. Happy, even. I think that frightens him. To his mind, gay is something scary, something Satan throws into people's paths to lead them astray."

"It's my life," George said. "And I worry about Satan just about as much as Dad does. Imaginary things can't hurt you."

"I'm sure of one thing," Karen added. "When Jim said he's never been with another woman, I'm pretty sure he was telling the truth. I have no doubt I'm the only one." She smiled briefly. "The only woman."

"Oooh," George commented. "But not..."

"I don't know. I have my suspicions, but I don't really know. I just know I've had enough."

"Can I leave now?" Carol asked.

"No," Susan said, rather sharply.

George looked at his parents. "You know, I get the impression you guys might need to be alone here."

Susan brushed that idea aside. "No, stay. I've dealt with this sort of thing before."

Ellen looked at her, her eyes wide. "Dad got someone pregnant before?"

Her mother laughed. "Only me, as far as I know. But he's had affairs."

"I'm not alone in this," Bob said. May as well get it all out in the open, he thought.

"Your glass is empty," Susan said. "You should probably go fill it."

"Good idea."

"And another for me, too."

"Of course." He took her empty glass and headed for the bar.

"You seem to be taking this whole thing pretty well, Mom," George said.

"Do I have a choice? If your father has an affair, I'll have one, too. We keep things pretty even, and we've been together for 40 years doing it just that way."

Ellen just managed to keep from dropping her glass. "Hey," she said, "we're all Dad's kids, right?"

"Of course you are," her mother declared.

"Right," George said. "If you were cheating, too…"

"Your father," Susan said, "is your father. Absolutely. No question about it."

Bob returned from the bar and handed his wife a fresh drink. "Here you are," he said.

"I think I need to talk to Karen," Eric said. "Is there someplace?"

"Use the kitchen," Susan suggested. "Lunch is going to be delayed anyway."

Bob watched his son's boyfriend and his daughter-in-law head off through the dining room toward the kitchen. He looked at his wife, and at his secretary—his mistress—sitting in his chair.

"What are *we* going to do?" he asked.

Susan stood up and nodded her head toward the door. "Outside." She looked at Carol. "You, too. Come on."

XV

THE SUN HAD GONE BEHIND A CLOUD and it was cooler on the porch. Carol felt a little left out. She was the only one not holding a drink. Well, she thought, she couldn't, could she? It might hurt the baby, and obviously she was going to keep it.

Obviously?

Yes, she thought, obviously. That was what choice was about, wasn't it? You either had the baby or you didn't, and it was your choice. The opposite idea, that there was no choice and if you got pregnant you had the baby whether you wanted to or—even if you knew it was going to kill you—didn't involve a choice. It involved compulsion.

Why is it "pro-life" if you're being forced to spend nine months carrying another person around inside you, but slavery if you're forced to spend nine months doing the same thing and the other person is in a sedan chair? Something for Bob to figure out, perhaps?

"You know," Carol said, "I never wanted to come between you two. Don't you?"

"You *are* a problem, aren't you?" Susan said.

"I suppose."

"Maybe we should find you a husband. Know anyone?"

"I can't think of anyone who'd be interested," Carol replied. "Not now, anyway."

"There's that problem," Susan agreed. "Still, I know a couple young men who might be looking. I could introduce you."

"How many of them are looking for a pregnant girl?"

"I suppose if he loved you," Bob said, "it wouldn't matter. There are even men who like the idea of an instant family. Though you do sometimes wonder if they're really interested in the mother, or just want to be a dad."

"You're not exactly encouraging her there, Bob. And the kid hasn't even been born yet. If she can find someone in the next couple weeks, she might even be able to convince him it was his kid."

Carol frowned. "Oh, that sounds *really* ethical. Still, I'm only about three weeks along. There's always a chance I could lose it. I hear slightly more than half of all pregnancies miscarry before the mother even knows she's pregnant, or very soon after."

Susan shook her head. "That's probably not going to happen to you."

"I'll be paying your expenses," Bob said. "Presuming I don't get fired."

"Yes, you are slightly in violation of policy, aren't you?"

Bob shrugged. "You know, I'm not actually sure. A superior dating a subordinate requires department head approval. I *am* the department head. And we weren't exactly dating, were we?"

"Well," Carol said, "you never bought me dinner. All we ever did was…"

"I can think of one possible solution," Susan said.

Bob raised an eyebrow. "What would that be?"

"I think you know," Susan said. "This is just such an unusual situation. I don't believe it's ever happened before. Not to us."

"I have no idea what you're talking about."

"Well, think about it, Bob. I told the kids no one else could be their father. I've had just as many affairs as you, but I still said that with absolute confidence it was true, didn't I?"

"Sure. You only fool around with other women. No chance you're getting pregnant that way."

Carol started edging toward the steps. "I'm beginning to feel a little uncomfortable here," she said, very quietly.

Bob looked at his wife, then at Carol.

"Oh." He nodded, then took a long swallow of his drink. "Right, that's something new."

"I may just lie down and die right here on the porch," Carol said.

"We do have a king-size bed," Susan said. "We could just put Carol in the middle."

"I can't even imagine," Bob mused, "what Jim would say if he found out we were both having an affair with the same woman at the same time."

"He'd tell us we're both going to hell."

"He's been telling me that all along."

"And now he'll include Carol and me."

"Are you two crazy?" Carol erupted. "I don't care about your idiot son, but what will the *college* say? They'd find out, you know. They're pretty liberal, but they are still run by a fucking church!"

"Possibly," Bob said, "we'll be retiring a little sooner than we expected."

"They make motor homes with king-size beds, too."

"The three of us? In the same bed? At the same time?"

"Well, for the first few weeks, maybe we can *both* cut Bob off. Probably serve him right."

"Hey!"

"Look," Carol said, "I'm not absolutely saying I wouldn't, but are you fucking nuts? Really? You want to move your husband's mistress into your house?"

"You're my lover, too," Susan said, sounding ridiculously practical. "That makes it a little more logical. Just think how convenient it would make things. No more sneaking around."

"It worked for Louis XV," Bob commented.

Carol just looked at him for a long moment. "You're not the king of France. And I'm not Madame Du Barry."

"I should hope not," Bob groaned. "She ended up with her head in a basket after the French Revolution."

"Look, I need to think about this. A lot."

"You should. I've never thought my wife was crazy before. Still, two at once…"

"Okay, I really do need to get home. I've got a lot of thinking to do. Lots and lots of thinking."

XVI

THEY WATCHED HER GO DOWN THE PORCH STEPS, out the front walk, and head down the street toward the west. She lived a block over, in the upstairs section of an old four square house that had been converted into a pair of full floor apartments.

"What do you think she'll decide?" Bob asked.

"I think this could work for her. She's right, it's a little strange, but in the long run? You and I are *not* splitting up. We both know that. And we obviously both care for her. So her child ends up with one father and two mothers, or a father, a mother, and an honorary aunt. It's cared for, anyway."

"Our existing children are going to think we've lost our minds."

"Except for Jim," Susan said. "He'll just think Satan's won and we're all damned. But I'm fairly sure he thinks that already."

"Oh, who gives a damn what he thinks?"

But what do *I* think? he wondered. Is this a stupid idea? Hell, if all three of us are in the same bed, will I even be able to perform? That's the sort of situation you see in porn, not in real life.

"You're not really both going to cut me off, are you?" he asked.

Susan laughed, sounding like a soprano Shadow. "We just might. Or, maybe it'll be just us girls playing and you get to watch and die of frustration with your hands tied to the headboard."

"You do that, too, wouldn't you?"

"Damn straight."

"Well, let's not say anything to the kids. George and Ellen don't need to know you've made this suggestion unless Carol decides she wants to do it. And she may not want to. After all, she's still a young, beautiful, sexy woman."

He suddenly realized he wasn't quite done with that thought. "And while you are, of course, a somewhat older, beautiful, sexy woman, I'm just... Well, I'm just old."

Susan brushed against him. "I hope she says 'yes.' The whole idea has me kind of tingly."

"Really? Tingly?"

She laughed. "Not a chance, Romeo. What I need right now is another drink."

"You go have your drink, then," he said, opening the door. "And I shall have the whole bloody bottle."